Dahlia in Bloom

Susan Koehler

Never be afraid to bloom. Susan Koehler

turtle cove press

ISBN 978-0-9859438-8-2

Library of Congress Control Number: 2019945716

Printed in the United States of America
The text of this book was typeset in Palatino Linotype.

Author photo by Hillary Koehler © 2019.
Cover photo of Dahlia by Katie Clark,
K.M. Clark Photography.
Cover design by Elizabeth Babski,
Babski Creative Studios.
Cover model (Emma T.) courtesy of
Making Light Productions, Tallahassee, Florida.

10 9 8 7 6 5 4 3 2 1 1 2 3 4 5 6 7 8 9 10

In memory of my mother

I

Can a person just decide to give up feeling scared? For as long as I could remember, I'd had a fear of snakes and thunder and my sister Celia when she's mad. Looking down from someplace way up high always gave me terrible jitters and made my belly jump up to my chest. But the worst kind of scared I knew was when Mommy's forehead got that worried wrinkle, and Poppy went hunting for squirrels 'cause meat was hard to come by and we had a lot of mouths to feed.

So I understood fear. What I did not understand was what I heard the day we walked from Zeke's cabin around the mountain to Pete Gaddy's store and gathered by the radio. That's when our new president said something that made no sense: *The only thing we have to fear is fear itself.*

Pete Gaddy shook his head and said, "Up here on the mountain, fear is what's keepin' most folks alive." I didn't know about that, but I knew that *fear itself* was not what scared me. It was snakes and thunder and high up places and going hungry. And Celia, of course.

I tried to ask my brother Charlie what he thought about the president's nonsense, but Charlie shushed me right away. He was caught up in a story Pete Gaddy was telling.

"You know," Pete said to Poppy, "folks say Ol' Zeke buried a treasure somewhere under that cabin of his."

He was talking about our home, of course. Ol' Zeke was my grandpap's uncle, and he built that cabin for him and his wife, Juliette. They'd been dead and gone more than a dozen years by the time I came along in 1924, but everyone on Harrell Mountain still called our place Zeke's Cabin.

Poppy looked at the dull wooden floorboards. He put his hands on his hips and shook his head back and forth. "That old story is just a bunch of foolishness," he said. "If Ol' Zeke had a-had him a treasure, it wouldn't make sense for him to bury it and go on a-livin' like poor folk."

Charlie wasn't looking at the floor, though. His eyes gazed upward like he could see that treasure spread out on the ceiling. I think he started making a plan right then and there to find Zeke's treasure. That's how come two weeks later I strolled outside and found him down on his hands and knees using an old ax blade to scrape out a tunnel by the base of the chimney.

"Poppy says it's just a bunch of foolishness," I reminded him. I rocked my little cornhusk doll in my arms, careful not to squeeze her brittle body too hard.

Charlie jabbed the ax blade into the cold, hard earth. "I'm tired of being poor," he said. "If I find that treasure, we won't sleep on straw bed-ticks in a one-room cabin. We'll live like Mr. John D. Rockefeller -- in a big mansion with a bunch of servants, fancy clothes, and all the food you can imagine. I'll even get you a store-bought doll. You mark my words, Dahlia!"

I hugged my cornhusk baby, knowing she wouldn't last much longer. She looked a far cry different from when Grandpap first twisted the dried husks and tied them together with twine. She sure was a comfort when I was sick and had to keep to the bed. But I couldn't help but imagine what a store-bought doll would feel like in my arms.

That's when an amazing notion sprang into my head: Mr. John D. Rockefeller probably didn't have anything to fear. He could just hide away inside his golden walls with all his trinkets and toys and never worry about being hungry. Best of all, if he didn't want to see some mean ol' ugly sister, he could just stay on his own side of the mansion and never have to look at her. With enough money, a person could buy away any reason they ever had to feel afraid.

"I reckon I could help you dig," I told Charlie. I leaned my cornhusk doll against the chimney and crouched by my brother, scraping dirt with my fingers. The ground was softer and more like soil several inches down. Ants scurried around in a panic and slick brown worms wiggled their way deeper into the dark ground.

"You need to stay back," he said. "You're only eight years old, and I don't wanna be blamed for you gettin' hurt or gettin' sick again."

"Eight and three quarters," I corrected him, and I spit in the dirt to make sure he knew I was serious.

He stopped for a minute and squinted at me. "Fussy and particular," he said. "That's how you got your name." He knew how to irritate me.

Mommy's favorite flowers were dahlias, so she planted them out in front of Zeke's cabin. They had big, colorful blossoms in the summer, but when cold weather came on, the plants all but disappeared. Mommy would say, "You just have to have faith. Those little dahlias will grow back and bloom again when the winter passes." Maybe they were particular, and she sure did fuss over them, but that's not why she called me Dahlia.

I spit again, a little closer to him this time. "Mommy told me I got my name because I was born in July when the beautiful dahlias were bursting into bloom."

"Believe what you want," he said, "but I know the truth." And he went back to digging.

It was clear that Charlie didn't want my help, so I backed away and brushed dirt from my hands. The March wind was a mix of warm and chill. I wrapped Mommy's old scarf around my neck in a couple of loops and tucked the ends into the top of my dress.

"I'm going for a walk," I said. He didn't even look up. I wasn't actually allowed to go off on my own, so I figured I'd just stroll all the way around the cabin, and maybe by the time I made it back to the chimney he'd be tired enough to let me help.

Zeke's cabin was tucked in a holler up in the Blue Ridge Mountains. The cabin was deeper than it was wide, and there were only a couple of windows on one side. It had a door on the front and a door on the back, kind of like bookends that held a bunch of stories in between. And the saddest story of all was about Ol' Zeke himself.

Zeke and Juliette had a little baby girl, and they named her Polly. Zeke built a pine cradle for that baby and carved little rose vines at each end of it. Juliette sewed a pink and white baby quilt with a shoo-fly pattern. Grandpap said a whole bunch of love was sewed into that quilt, but even all that love couldn't protect little Polly. A sickness stole through the mountain, and Juliette and little Polly both came down with a terrible fever. The baby faded out of this world in just a few days' time.

Zeke dug that baby a grave in the cold ground of the family cemetery. He turned that beautiful cradle into a coffin and buried little Polly in it. Then he got on his knees at Juliette's bedside and promised the Lord all sorts of things if He'd just let her live. Well, she did live, but they never had any more children. They plowed a small field in the clearing out in front of the cabin and just kept to themselves mostly.

Juliette hadn't come from this mountain. Her people lived over near Jefferson, but nobody knew much about them. All I knew was Zeke married her and brought her back to Harrell Mountain. He built that cabin for her, and who knows, maybe he buried a treasure under it.

I eased around the corner to where Charlie was digging and spotted my cornhusk doll leaning against the chimney, spattered with loose dirt. I cleared my throat as I moved closer, but Charlie never looked up. He just kept jabbing that ax blade into the earth and dragging out mounds of dirt. I opened my mouth to speak but never got the words out. Because that's when it happened.

Clink. Charlie's blade hit something solid and we both froze.

II

We can't get too excited yet," Charlie told me. But he was breathing mighty fast and his hands were shaking. "Come over here and help me widen out this tunnel."

I dropped the doll and fell to my knees. We both paddled our hands like a couple of dogs after a bone. Something white and shiny peeked up at us. "Just keep making the hole wider," Charlie said. As we did, a few other shiny white spots appeared.

"All right, stand back now. I'll pry it up with the ax blade," Charlie announced. He gently slid the sharp metal under the edge of the solid object. He rocked back and forth, trying to work it loose from the soil.

All at once, Charlie tumbled onto his bottom in a mound of dirt, and our white mystery popped loose, landing at my feet.

I beheld our treasure. An old broken plate.

We were brushing the dirt off our hands when a skinny shadow came creeping up behind us. It blocked the little bit of light that was easing into

Charlie's tunnel and shattered our morning's peace.

"Does Mommy know you two have that ax blade?" Celia was standing there with her arms crossed and her foot tapping, trying to look like she was grown instead of just eighteen miserable months older than me and four whole years younger than Charlie. She had a long red ribbon in her hair, and it was tied up into a lopsided bow. She sure thought she was somebody.

"Poppy gave me the ax blade so I could fix up a new handle for it," Charlie said. "Not that it's any of your business." I liked it when he talked to her that way. And I was jealous of the fact he could get away with it.

"Well, Poppy's off at Hugh Spicer's place helping plant some fruit trees. Heaven knows those good-for-nothing Spicer boys won't be any help." Celia put her hands on her hips and directed her orders at Charlie. "Mommy says you need to head over to Grandpap's and help him with his spring garden."

Charlie stood up straight, his long morning shadow stretching away from Celia. He walked off toward Grandpap's cabin without another word, and I wished I could go with him.

"And Dahlia," Celia snapped, "Rae and I have to

go fetch some water from the spring. I'm sure there's something useful you could be doing instead of playing in the dirt."

I followed Celia inside the dark cabin and blinked my eyes hard a few times, trying to force them to adjust. Mommy was standing over her wood stove, too busy to notice us. After hanging my scarf on a peg by the door, I headed to the back wall and plopped down on the bed I shared with Rae and Celia.

Poppy made our bed frames out of poplar wood and Mommy sewed the bed ticks out of flour sacks. Every fall, we stuffed them with straw left over from the wheat and rye after it had been thrashed. They looked like big soft clouds and you had to climb up on them. After a while, though, they flattened out and you could feel the bedrails under your back. I understood why Charlie hated them.

I heard whispering and turned my eyes to see Celia standing by the stove with her hands on her hips again. "Mommy, I was barely seven years old when I had to start helping with the water. Dahlia's comin' up on nine and she's never had to help."

"I don't want her a-gettin' too cold," Mommy whispered back.

"The wind's dying down and the sun's gettin'

warm," Celia argued. "It would be good for her to do a little work."

"We just can't be too careful." Mommy turned and looked at me with that fretful expression she'd been wearing ever since the doctor said the word *diphtheria*. It had been over two months since I came down with that terrible sickness, and I hadn't been back to school since.

It all started with a sore throat, but then I got a fever that just hung on. Mommy kept me in bed and tended to me for two days, but on the third day they put me in the wagon and hauled me to town.

The old white-haired doctor gave me a shot and told Mommy to keep me off by myself. Then he made all the other children in the family get shots, too. Celia was still mad about that.

Mommy mumbled something I couldn't make out, and then Rae joined the conversation. I leaned in close and heard Rae say, "We could start teaching her what to do. I'll keep an eye on her, Mommy." Rae was only twelve, but she sure did act grown up.

Mommy turned, and this time her face was serious. She nodded at me and said, "All right. Dahlia, you go and help your sisters fetch some water. I've got a stew to put together." Knowing better than to argue, I stood up and tried to ignore the knot in my stomach.

Rae picked up the five-gallon milk keg we used for water. It was made of metal and covered with brown wood slats around the middle. She whisked it out the door with Celia and me following right behind, except Celia stopped in the doorway. She whipped her head around and glared at me with her little ol' weasel eyes.

Even though my insides were twisted up, I glared right back at her. She turned on her heel and stuck her pointy nose up in the air. When she did, that lopsided red ribbon slipped out of her dirt-colored hair and dropped silently onto the wood floor. Served her right. I picked it up and tucked it away in my dress pocket, figuring I'd give it back to her when she was a little less ornery.

The walk down to the spring was easy. The keg was empty, and after we got up out of the holler, the path led downhill mostly. Songbirds whistled melodies, the air was cool without being cold, and sunlight trickled through the trees like raindrops. Dogwood buds on their pale branches looked like they were floating in the air.

When we reached the spring Rae said, "Dahlia, stay back and just watch. I don't want you gettin' close to the water." Rae was pretty tall, and she always kept her blonde hair cut short. It made her look kind of serious, so it was easy to do as she said.

Clear water came out of a hole and ran off a level piece of stone. It poured into a shallow stream that wound on down the mountain. Rae planted one foot on a tree root, and her other foot was balanced on a rock. While she leaned down and held the mouth of that keg under the icy cold water, I held my breath and tried not to think about what might happen if she slipped in and got carried off.

At a certain point, Rae's arms started to tremble, and her face got all pinched up. She hollered, "Celia, come grab ahold!"

Instead of running to help, Celia jumped up so close to me that her long dark hair blew into my face. She whispered, "You need to grow up. Grab ahold of that keg and help."

Without time to think, I ran and slipped my hands around the wooden slats. Rae shouted, "Grab it underneath!" She was generally real soft-spoken, and I wasn't used to hearing her yell. I slid my hands under the keg as fast as I could, trying to keep my fingers from trembling.

I felt for something solid to brace one foot against, but when I did, my other foot slipped through the slick mud. My hands let go of the keg, and I was suddenly flat on my back in the cold, shallow water.

Celia managed to wedge herself under the keg so it didn't tumble into the stream. Neither one of them looked at me, but I heard Rae holler, "Get out of that water, Dahlia! You'll catch your death of cold, and we'll be in trouble for it."

I scooted myself up to dry land. My entire backside was soaked, and water dripped off me about as fast as it came out of that spring. I turned to watch the stream wind its way down the mountain, and my heart sank when I noticed that the contents of my pocket had slipped away into the rolling water. Thankfully, Celia was too busy to see her precious red ribbon being carried downstream.

Once the keg was full, they set it on the ground. "Let me check out the damage," Rae said, sounding a little irritated. She wrung out the back of my dress while I watched water pool around my feet.

Celia frowned and stood with her arms crossed. "We're not gonna be able to wring all the water out, Rae. We'll have to find a sunny spot to let her dry."

Rae raised her eyebrows. "That's not a bad idea," she said. "Dahlia, let's walk up to the flat rock, and lay you out in the sunshine."

The flat rock was a big slab of stone where we

always had our Easter picnic. "We'll take a little rest while you get dry," Rae said. Then she added, "And let's not mention any of this to Mommy."

I agreed to keep it a secret. Celia told me I needed to cross my heart and hope to die, but Rae said that wasn't necessary.

We took turns holding the keg, two at a time, as we walked up from the spring. I never knew water could weigh so much. When we finally reached the flat rock, Rae told me to stretch out on my belly and let the sun dry the back of my dress. The rock was hard but warm, and the soft breeze whispered in my ears and ran across my back.

My sisters sat down, and for a few minutes, we just listened to the rustling of leaves and the rippling of water off in the distance. Then, out of the near silence, Celia started to sing one of those sad old mountain songs that Mommy liked to sing.

"No home, no home, cried a little girl
At the door of a rich man's home
As she feebly leaned on a marble wall
And stood on a polished stone."

I'll be darned if she didn't sound pretty good, but I wouldn't dare tell her so. Rae and I joined, and soon we had sung a bunch of those old songs.

We were having some fun until Rae got nervous and said we'd better head home. She touched the back of my dress to make sure it was mostly dry. Rae and Celia toted the water keg the rest of the way, and we walked so fast nobody was able to say another word.

When we got home, Mommy's face was screwed up tight in an angry frown. "Dahlia, you don't need to be a-helpin' if you're just gonna slow 'em down!" she snapped. "Your Grandpap's a-comin' for supper, so set an extra place at the table."

Rae and Celia didn't say a word. They rushed around to set the table and then hurried outside to watch for Grandpap.

"Can I help you?" I asked.

"It would be best if you'd just stay out of my way and let me concentrate."

I sat down at the table and watched Mommy work. Her light brown hair was twisted back behind her head. A thick strand had come loose, and she kept shoving it out of her face.

The stew was cooking in a big iron pot, and I reckon it was getting mighty dry. Mommy added some water and stirred real fast. Then she threw a couple handfuls of flour in her dough bowl. She poured in some buttermilk, scooped up a little lard, and shook a few drops of that spring water off her fingertips. Her hands moved so fast it was hard for my eyes to keep up.

She kneaded it into a soft dough and then pinched off pieces to make biscuits. Once they were in the oven, Mommy heated some water and started scrubbing her dough bowl. She sure did work to keep things clean.

Finally, she looked over to the table where I was sitting. She wiped her hands on her apron and sighed real loud. She poured a glass of buttermilk and handed me a piece of leftover cornbread to crumble in it.

"This oughta hold you 'til supper. As soon as I pull the biscuits out of the oven, I'm a-goin' to the cow shed to milk Ol' Rosie." For just a moment, she stood still, and I noticed that worried wrinkle on her forehead. But then she gave my shoulders a little squeeze. "The stove is hot, so don't go a-touchin' it."

Soon enough I heard the cabin door creak open and bounce back with a soft thud. I was alone. The afternoon sun was starting to melt down onto the mountaintops, and a peaceful glow filled the cabin. But that peace disappeared as soon as the door swung open and Celia burst into the room. "I know

I had it when we went to fetch the water, Rae!"

Rae followed, trying to calm her down. "It could have slipped out while we were walking," she said. "That ribbon could be anywhere."

Celia stopped right next to me and crossed her arms tight over her chest. "Or somebody spiteful could have taken it," she said.

"I don't know what you're talking about," I lied. Celia squinted her eyes and kept them glued on me for a long while before she finally turned away. Then that old sun crawled a little lower and long afternoon shadows crept across the cabin.

III

When the sound of Grandpap's whistle danced into the holler, I was glad for the distraction. All eyes darted to the door, even though we knew there'd be no surprise. If there was one thing you could count on about Grandpap, it was that you always knew what to expect. There was so much sameness about that man.

He always wore a white dress shirt and faded overalls that were so worn out they felt as soft and smooth as a rose petal. His thin white hair was never out of place, and there was never a wrinkle in his clothes. When he appeared in the doorway, that's just exactly what we saw. Except for one thing.

Grandpap's big ol' feather-bed sack was slung over his shoulder. It was like a giant white quilt with goose feathers stuffed inside. When he folded it into a long skinny column and carried it with him, we knew he was planning on sleepin' out.

Charlie joined him a bunch of times, and even

Rae and Celia slept out with Grandpap a time or two. I was the only one who'd never spent the night in the holler under the stars. It sent shivers down my spine to think of being out on the ground in the dark night.

Mommy's voice woke me out of my daydreaming. I hadn't seen her slip in behind Grandpap and that feather bed. "What'd you do with my boy, Pap?"

"He decided to stay outside and watch for John," Grandpap answered. If Charlie was outside, I knew it didn't have anything to do with waiting for Poppy.

"Can I go and wait with Charlie?" I asked.

"As long as there's not a chill," Mommy answered.

I slipped out into the warm sunlight. It crawled flat over the clearing and just reached the young dahlia shoots stretching up out of the soil. But Charlie was nowhere in sight. I eased around the side of the cabin and found him hunched in the shadows that rested on the chimney.

"Charlie," I whispered. He nearly jumped out of his skin.

"You shouldn't come sneakin' up on a person, Dahlia," he scolded. "But since you're here, stand at the corner and watch for Poppy. Give me a warning when he gets close."

I tiptoed over to the corner but kept my eyes on Charlie. He was flinging loose dirt toward the chimney and it was landing on my cornhusk doll. A few pieces had broken off her brittle body and splotches of mildew were forming on what was left of her head. *Who needs a silly old doll anyway*, I thought. But inside, my heart felt a little bit heavy.

"Do you really believe there's a treasure, Charlie?" I turned to look across the clearing.

Charlie's voice came at me muffled and out of breath, but I understood him just fine. "The way I see it, that broken plate was a sign. I surely do believe Zeke buried something, and since the cabin was already standing when he did it, the treasure's got to be near one of the walls." I'd never heard my brother sound so sure of himself.

Just then, I saw the top of Poppy's old brown hat bobbing up and down in the distance. "He's coming," I whispered.

Charlie jumped up, brushing dirt from his hands and pants. He crept up behind me and asked, "Can we just keep this between us?"

I turned and looked him straight in the eyes. "As long as you'll let me help."

"It's a deal." And we shook on it.

We walked out into the clearing to greet Poppy. His blue eyes looked almost gray in the fading light, and even though his hands were empty, his shoulders were hunched over like he was carrying something heavy. "Tell your mother to come outside for a minute. There's something I need to discuss with her in private."

We did as he asked but left the door open just enough to peek through the crack. We couldn't hear Poppy, but we saw Mommy's worried wrinkle deepen. As he talked, Poppy reached out and put a gentle hand on her elbow. She took a few deep breaths like she was trying to push the worry away. She looked at the ground and nodded.

"What're you young'uns spying on?" Grandpap's voice startled us, and we scattered. It was just in time, too, 'cause that door opened almost as soon as we cleared away from it.

Mommy followed Poppy inside and the floorboards creaked under their heavy footsteps. Poppy sat down in his old straight-back chair at the head of the table. "Children, gather 'round," he said. "Your mother and I have something to tell you." We lined up around the table. Poppy went on to say that times were hard and he was afraid they wouldn't get better any way soon.

"Ol' Duel Walker's son Dwight is in town. He sold some trees to Hugh Spicer and I went down to lend Hugh a hand with 'em." Poppy looked at the table but raised his eyebrows hopefully. "Well, Mr. Walker got to talkin' and he made me an offer I can't refuse." He paused for just a minute and looked at us one by one.

"Besides being a traveling salesman," Poppy continued, "Mr. Walker has a big farm over in Lothian Mill. He needs someone to run the farm for him since he's away so much, and he's offered us the chance to live and work at his place for a while."

My mouth got real dry and my legs trembled. I leaned against Grandpap to keep from falling. He was stiff as a board and just as silent, too. We'd never lived anywhere but Harrell Mountain. How could we just up and leave?

Rae and Celia had locked arms like they were trying to anchor themselves down. From across the table, I watched Charlie's face go from excited to desperate in an instant. And I understood. How could he ever find the treasure if we had to leave Zeke's cabin?

"There's a house we can live in, a school you children can go to, and enough work to keep us all busy. In exchange, we can live in that house for no cost, and eat from what we raise. If things go well, we may even earn a little cash money. I've thought it over, and I've decided it's the right thing to do."

Charlie was the first one to speak. "But this is our home, Poppy. And there are things we need to take care of right here." I'd never seen him cry before, but he had wet eyes and a little crackle in his voice.

Mommy patted his back and said, "Ol' Zeke's cabin has been around for a long time, and it'll still be here when things get better."

"What about Ol' Rosie?" Rae asked. I hadn't even given a thought to Mommy's milk cow.

"There's not room to take her with us now," Poppy said, "but Mr. Walker says we can head back and get her by and by." Then he turned to Grandpap. "Pap, 'you think you could look after her for a bit?"

Grandpap crossed his arms and said, "Looks like I don't have a choice."

"How much time do we have?" Charlie asked.

Poppy and Charlie looked at each other for a long minute. Finally, Poppy said, "Spring planting season is a-slippin' away. Dwight Walker has a huckster truck that'll carry all of us and a fair amount of cargo. He'll be here in the morning to pick us up."

Charlie jumped up from the table and walked straight outside. Mommy called after him, but Poppy said, "Let the boy get a little air, Mary. He'll be all right."

Poppy said the blessing, and we ate in near silence. The only sounds were the rattling of spoons against bowls and a loud sigh from Grandpap every once in a while.

Finally, when the biscuits were gone and the stew was just about finished, Charlie came back inside with dirt on his hands and disappointment in his eyes. "Sit and eat your stew," Poppy said. "We've got a long night ahead of us."

That's when Grandpap spoke. "I'll be a-sleepin' out tonight." He leaned back in his chair and crossed his arms. "Any of you young'uns want to join me? It might be your last chance."

"For cryin' out loud," Poppy said, "this is just temporary." He stared at Grandpap long and hard, but Grandpap refused to look at Poppy.

"No takers?" Charlie and Rae didn't say a word, and Celia turned her pointy nose up and looked away.

I don't know what possessed me to do it, but I

shouted, "I'd like to sleep out, Grandpap!" He gave me a sad-looking grin, and then raised his eyebrows toward Mommy.

Mommy looked down at her bowl and said, "It's nowhere near warm enough for such a thing. I can't let that girl get sick again."

"It's unseasonably warm this evenin'," Grandpap replied. "And a little fresh air might do the child some good."

Then Poppy added his two cents. "We've got a lot of work to do tonight. Might be easier this way."

Mommy let out a sigh and closed her eyes. "Are you sure you won't get scared?" she asked me. "Once you get out under those trees, there won't be any turnin' back."

"I've already been all the way to the spring to help with the water," I reminded her. Celia nearly spit out a mouthful of milk when I said that. I made a point of ignoring her. "And," I continued, "being out in the nighttime is no different from being out in the day. I won't be scared." I hoped that saying that would make it true.

"Well, I reckon it'll be all right," Mommy said. "You carry somethin' to keep you warm."

I grabbed a quilt and followed Grandpap out into the misty twilight. His feather bed was draped

tried to squeeze my eyes shut, but they popped open when Grandpap took a deep breath and spoke one more time. "Don't be afraid." He lifted a long, skinny finger and pointed it straight up toward that owl. "He's a-watchin' over us."

I didn't want to be scared, but those big yellow eyes watching over us brought no peace to my soul. I don't know how long it was until my eyes were finally able to close in sleep.

That next morning, I woke up with the first small whispers of sunlight. When the dew covered the ground, it decided to go ahead and cover me, too. My hair felt moist and sticky against my forehead. I was trying to move my neck, but it ached at just the thought of moving. My eyes roved through the trees and searched for that owl. Thankfully, he was nowhere in sight. I forced myself to stand, damp and achy to the bones, and wound my quilt up in my arms.

From the corner of my eye, I saw Grandpap wandering through the fruit trees off toward his cabin. He must've heard me moving.

"Looks like it'll be a good year for peaches!" he hollered. Grandpap loved his peaches. Every summer, he cut them in half and put them into Mason jars full of thick, sweet syrup. He turned each peach so that the blushing pink side faced out and made sure both sides of the jar looked exactly the same.

"Yum!" I shouted, hoping we'd be back home by the time the peaches were ripe. Surely, we would.

Grandpap turned and walked toward me. He picked up his feather bed, shook it out, and folded it over four times into that long skinny column. He took one more look around, nodded, and then said, "We'd better get to walkin'. Your folks will be a-lookin' for you soon."

As we plodded along, my heart was already missing him. I didn't want to go. What would I do without Grandpap, and the mountain, and Zeke's cabin? I'd feel tossed about like a little bird in a storm.

And then I thought about the treasure. It was our only hope. I just had to ask. "Grandpap, do you think there's really a treasure buried under Zeke's cabin?"

He laughed a little, and his blue eyes narrowed. "Well, now, that story's been a-goin' around for many a-year. What do you think?"

"Charlie said if he could find that treasure, we could live like the Rockefellers," I told him.

Grandpap stopped walking, and he stopped

smiling. "Charlie's got a restless soul," he said. "That boy needs to find his peace."

Then he fixed his eyes on the path back to Zeke's cabin and started moving forward again. I knew there was no more point in talking. I wrapped the quilt around my shoulders and we walked side by side. Birds chattered above us and twigs crackled under our feet. A cool breeze kicked up against our backs and pushed us toward home.

When we reached the holler, we both stopped in our tracks. No smoke curled from the chimney and no scent of coffee or biscuits drifted on the breeze. All the world seemed still except for a dark green huckster truck winding its way toward our home.

IV

Dwight Walker parked his truck on the side of the road, so we had to carry our belongings up out of the holler and across Poppy's fallow cornfield.

"You girls wipe your feet and then pile up in that back seat," Mommy told us.

Mr. Walker had fixed up a small wooden bench behind the main seat. It was mighty narrow, and I was squeezed tight in the middle between Rae and Celia.

Mommy gave us a couple of quilts to hold in our laps. "These'll keep you warm in case you get a chill, and we'll save some space in the truck bed." She let out a nervous sigh but tried to smile through it.

We stayed huddled up together, but every once in a while, we'd see them coming with another load. Baskets and bags filled the floor behind us, and Mommy's old rocker was balanced on the top. The whole truck shook when Poppy and Mr. Walker hopped up and dragged our table and chairs into the back. They tied it all up with rope while we just waited, squished together, silent and curious.

When they finally finished, Charlie squeezed into the front seat along with the grown-ups. He was fourteen years old and nearly as big as a full-grown man, but he looked like he was sitting halfway on Mommy's lap, which made us giggle. He tried to turn around and shame us, but Poppy said, "Sit still, son."

As we drove away, the warm sun was just sneaking up and turning the windshield into a mirror. I saw Mommy's reflection staring at the road, lips pressed together real tight, no doubt pining about leaving Ol' Rosie and the chickens behind.

Poppy's head bobbed back and forth like he was trying to see something he might have left behind. His face was long and heavy, and even the wrinkles on his forehead seemed to be frowning. I half-thought we might turn around right then and there, but that didn't happen.

We rode and rode for a long, bumpy time that day. The weariest part of it was the narrow dirt roads and winding turns in the mountains. Once we got to the highway, the sun was up and our ride seemed easy. The scenery moved along like a picture-lullaby. I don't even remember drifting off to sleep, but I must have. When I woke up, there was drool dried to the right side of my mouth, and my head had a sore spot from where it was leaning against Celia's bony shoulder.

I heard Mr. Walker telling Mommy that his wife was pleased about us coming. "I think Bessie gets lonesome for company sometimes," he said. "She's got the church on Sunday mornings, but most of the week I'm either off sellin' or I'm out workin' in the fields. The children are with her, of course, but they don't stand still long enough for conversation. I think she'll like having another woman to talk to."

So, they have children, I thought. I hadn't considered that. Just in the nick of time, I saw a bright red cardinal and made a wish on it that they wouldn't be mean as the dickens. We already had one of those, and one is enough.

Mr. Walker was still talking. "Bessie's gonna have a big dinner waitin' for us." He lifted his head and sniffed at the air a couple of times. "I think I'm starting to smell that cornbread, okra, and fried chicken already!"

Poppy laughed and said, "Dwight, I believe your nose is even stronger than mine. I can only smell the cornbread from here." I sniffed and sniffed, but I couldn't smell anything but Celia's rosewater perfume.

It wasn't long before we turned off the highway and worked our way down some smaller roads. There were split rail fences, chicken coops, cows, and wide-open fields on both sides of the highway. Pretty soon we came to a post office, and above the door I noticed a white wooden sign with blue letters painted on it. Mr. Walker announced, "Here we are in Lothian Mill!" I shook Rae and Celia until they were good and awake.

Rae kept her head turned toward one side of the truck while Celia watched out the other side. They were naming everything they saw, from a general store, to a barbershop, to a church with two red doors on the front. It was right after the church that we made a sharp turn to the right and Mr. Walker announced we were almost there.

The truck slowed down and rolled along a fairly smooth dirt road past a couple of wood-frame houses and a barn on Rae's side. On Celia's side, there was a real steep hill covered with rocks, red clay, and creeping vines.

"Everything you see on this side of the road is my property, John. I have a few people working for me, but they don't know the land like you do. You just tell 'em what to do though, and they'll do it."

We turned onto a smooth clay path. On the right, there was a hill running up to the biggest beech tree I'd ever seen. Behind the beech tree was a two-story house made of unpainted wood. It was bigger than our cabin, but much smaller than the white house over to our left. That house looked to be three stories tall, and just about as wide as it was high. It had a porch that stretched all the way across the front and wrapped around both sides. Out front, there was a pump coming up out of the ground for drawing water.

Mr. Walker turned toward the big white house, and out Celia's side I could see a barn, some sheds, and a group of wood-fenced animal pens. Back behind the unpainted house and animal pens, there was a row of sprawling oak trees alongside rows and rows of apple trees. Grandpap would like that, I thought. Of course, he'd want to add some peach trees to it.

Between the houses and the road, there were fields – just long, flat fields. In the golden afternoon, they seemed to stretch right out into the sky. Halfway between the two houses was a building with no walls -- just a roof propped up on wooden poles. Poppy saw it too. "I bet that pole barn comes in handy," he said.

The truck suddenly jolted to a stop and I held my breath, not knowing whether I wanted to step out or hide under the pile of quilts. Poppy and Charlie got out and stretched, watching Mr. Walker like they were trying to pick up a clue about which way to move or what to say. Mommy straightened her apron and fidgeted with her collar.

Suddenly, a sing-songy voice broke the silence. It was sweet and gentle like a chickadee, coming from the direction of the big house. As the voice grew closer, we realized it was coming from a round, smiling woman trotting toward us through the stringy grass. She had short gray hair framing her cheery face and wore a white apron over her long skirt, just like Mommy. "Welcome, welcome!" she shouted. "Let me see those children!"

Poppy helped Celia out, and Mommy motioned for us to follow. She smiled, but her face looked a little nervous. Rae and Celia were loaded down with quilts, so that friendly woman reached her arms out and came straight for me. She wrapped me up in her big softness and squeezed me tight.

Next she hugged Rae and Celia too and then wrapped her arms around Mommy. "I'm Mrs. Walker, but folks call me Miss Bessie."

Before we knew it, she scooped us all up and swept us toward the house. Setting foot on the whitewashed porch steps, we could smell something warm and delicious.

Mr. Walker swung open the front door, and we realized that the fried chicken, okra, and cornbread he promised were just the beginning. Two big baskets sat on the long kitchen table and both were filled with fresh biscuits. In between the baskets were jars of pickles and jellies. There was even a bowl of peanut butter. It was a feast!

Three boys and one girl, all scrubbed clean and lined up like stair-steps, stood along the far side of the table. The biggest one looked just like Mr. Walker with short, dark hair and a gentle face. The two boys beside him were almost the same height. They both had brown hair, freckled cheeks, and devilish grins. But the one who caught my attention was the girl. I noticed right away that she was about my size. She had curly, chestnut-colored hair and big brown eyes that danced all around like jumping beans, but she acted all shy and tried to hide behind her brothers. Miss Bessie introduced them from the tallest to the smallest as Dwight Jr., Wayne, Hoyt, and Ruby.

Mr. Walker and Miss Bessie sat down in the

chairs at each end of the table, and the rest of us squeezed together on benches along the sides. After a long, thankful blessing, we stuffed ourselves to the brim with that delicious food while the grown-ups did a bunch of talking. Then Mr. Walker picked up a lantern and led us through the darkness to the unpainted house that would be our home.

V

"You children remember, this house doesn't belong to us. We're just a-stayin' while we build up a little money." Mommy must've said that ten times a day. But the truth is, after a few weeks, Zeke's cabin seemed like something from a dream. The big unpainted house was real. We could touch its rough planks and knobby nails and smell its oak and pine.

The downstairs was split in two by a staircase. On one side, there was a good-sized kitchen with a wood stove and a wide-open space for our table and chairs. On the other side, there was a little parlor room for no real purpose. "Just for a-sittin' and a-visitin'," Poppy said.

There were two bedrooms upstairs. Mommy and Poppy settled in one of them, and the other was for Rae, Celia, and me. Our room had soft cotton mattresses, a straight-back chair angled in the corner, and a chest of drawers with a foggy mirror on top of it.

Charlie slept in the attic on an iron bed, right

under the peak of the roof. There was no other furniture -- just raw wood, cobwebs, and a little square window that looked out on the beech tree. After just a few days, he made a stool out of some scrap wood and set it by the window.

I didn't know how to bring it up to Charlie, but it seemed to me like maybe we'd stumbled into a little bit of treasure accidentally. Maybe we didn't need to dig up a whole lot – just enough for some walls, doors, and cotton mattresses of our own. I missed Grandpap and the mountain, but even Charlie had to realize there were some good things about that unpainted house on the Walkers' farm.

One of my favorite things was Ruby. On our first morning there, Miss Bessie showed up bright and early with a basket full of ham and biscuits. Curly-headed Ruby was at her side. Her roundish brown eyes looked right into mine, and it was like we decided we'd be friends, because from that day on, that's just what we were.

For the rest of spring and into the summer, time moved quickly. Poppy got the fields plowed, planted, and growing strong. Charlie was at his side, but there were a few other farm hands, too. Once school was out, Ruby's brothers joined in for a few hours each day. Back home, the fields were a whole lot smaller, but Poppy and Charlie did all the work by themselves.

Rae followed Mommy around and started acting like a grown woman. When she wasn't helping with the cleaning or cooking, she was practicing her sewing. Miss Bessie gave her a little wicker sewing basket, and that thing dangled from Rae's elbow everywhere she went. Whenever she got a chance, she was piecing together quilt squares.

Mommy made quilts from scraps, but they were just odd shapes sewn together and tacked with knots. Miss Bessie made quilts that looked like stained-glass windows. She taught Rae to piece together beautiful patterns with names like *log cabin, pinwheel star,* and even *shoo-fly,* like in that old story about Zeke and Juliette.

Celia buzzed around like an old June bug with no place to land. Rae tried to teach her to sew, but Celia didn't have the patience for it. Sometimes she played with Ruby and me, but that never lasted long. She'd get irritated, turn her nose up, and stomp away.

Mostly, we played with Lucille. That's what Ruby named the store-bought baby doll she got for her eighth birthday. Lucille's body was made out of cloth and stuffed with soft cotton. Her head was stiff, made out of something Ruby called celluloid. Big brown eyes were painted above her little molded nose and pink cheeks. Brown curls peeked out from under her lacy bonnet, and she wore a pink gingham dress. That doll even had real shoes – shiny and black – that were stuck to her feet with glue.

Ruby was real nice to share her doll with me. We sat on the front porch and rocked Lucille, sang lullabies to her, and pretended to feed her. When we got tired of playing with Lucille, we put her in her little wooden cradle and covered her with a tiny quilt Miss Bessie made.

For some reason, just the sight of Lucille made Celia irritable. She liked to say, "Only babies play with baby dolls," and then run off. The only thing Celia seemed to like to do for any piece of time was ride on that split wood swing hanging from the big beech tree. She liked it with Charlie best of all. They'd each stand on one side and pump their knees up and down until they were flying high enough to see way down Salem Road.

One day Celia begged me to stop playing with Ruby and come swing with her. "I need somebody to pump the other side of that piece of wood. Please, Dahlia. It's fun! You'll see."

She looked pitiful. "Oh, all right," I told her. "I'll do it if you promise we won't go any higher than the edge of the roof."

"Fine!" Celia said in a huff, and she hopped on one side of the board. I climbed carefully onto the other side, holding tight to the rope. We rocked back and forth in the shade of that tall tree while Ruby sat on the front porch holding Lucille.

At first it was all right, but as we moved faster, my head got dizzy and my heart was thumping so hard I could feel it in my ears. Just about the time we could see the rooftop, I quit pumping, thinking we'd coast until we could drag our feet in the dirt and stop that crazy swing.

Celia had a different idea. When I stopped pumping, she pumped harder. That swing carried us up toward the big branches and wobbled crooked with a little slack in the rope. "Celia, stop!" I yelled.

Over the rooftop, I saw the rows of apple trees way off behind the house. Suddenly, I felt like somebody pulled the floor out from under me. The whole world was spinning. I squeezed my eyes shut, but that made it worse. I gripped that rope so tight my fingers stung like they were on fire.

Then I heard Ruby's voice yell, "Celia, slow it

down!"

And she did. She dragged her feet across the dry, dusty ground while I squeezed the rope with cramped and burning hands.

"Baby!" Celia shouted, and then she walked off behind the house. A swarm of angry bees filled my insides, buzzing and stinging and making a fuss. I let out a savage holler and sat down on the porch next to Ruby. She slipped her arm around my shoulders and put Lucille in my lap.

"What's all this belly-aching out here?" Rae stepped through the screen door and put her hands on her hips.

"Celia's mean!" I whimpered.

Rae was quiet for a minute, and then she said, "Are you just now figuring that out?" She busted out laughing, and so did Ruby. Pretty soon, my sobs turned into giggles and one by one, those little angry bees flew away.

"You don't know how good you have it," Rae said. "You're out here swinging and playing with baby dolls. Charlie's working in the fields, I'm inside doing chores, and Mommy just sent that mean sister of yours out to collect eggs."

I looked down at Lucille. "I'm sorry. I hadn't thought about that."

Rae answered over her shoulder as she headed back to the kitchen. "Enjoy being the baby while you can. It won't last forever."

Ruby sat up straight and her brown eyes danced with excitement. "Wait a minute! Your birthday is Independence Day, right?"

I nodded.

"Well, that's just a couple of weeks away! We always have a big picnic for Independence Day. This year we can have a birthday party! I'll go ask my Momma!" And with that, Ruby grabbed Lucille and ran off, leaving me alone with my thoughts on the porch of that unpainted house.

Back on the mountain, the dahlias would tell me my birthday was coming. They'd burst into bloom and announce that it was about time for Mommy to make my seven-layer cake. Grandpap would come down to the cabin, and they'd all sing to me. Then we'd eat that cake, and if Poppy had a little cash money, he'd walk me over to Pete Gaddy's store for a peppermint stick.

But there were no dahlias on the Walkers' farm. Pete Gaddy's store was a far-off memory, and Grandpap was someone I was working hard not to forget.

❋ ❋ ❋

Just before 2:00 on Independence Day, we marched toward the pole barn carrying a whole mess of biscuits, a big pot of beans, and best of all, a seven-layer cake. Like always, Mommy's dress was covered by an apron, and Rae's sewing basket swung from her elbow.

We saw Mr. Walker and his boys coming toward us with turnip greens, corn on the cob, sliced tomatoes, and a great big ham. Miss Bessie trotted along behind them with two pitchers of sweet iced tea.

Ruby had a brand-new skipping rope, so we all took turns with it. Rae was pretty good! Charlie had made his own bow and arrows, and he brought them to the picnic to shoot with Ruby's brothers.

"Please, Papa, please!" Wayne and Hoyt jumped up and down begging Mr. Walker to let them shoot arrows with Charlie.

"As long as you aim away from the pole barn and the girls, you can shoot all you like," Mr. Walker told them. Then he leaned over to his oldest boy and said, "Dwight Jr., you keep an eye on them."

That day we filled our bellies with food, and we

laughed and played like we had no worries. When the afternoon started to fade, it was finally time to share the seven-layer cake. And that's when I got some special surprises. Miss Bessie gave me some chalk and a slate, "so you can practice gettin' ready for school," she said. Mommy gave me a small quilt, just about two feet long, and I couldn't figure out what I was supposed to do with it at first.

Then Rae reached down in her sewing basket and pulled out the most wonderful gift of all. It was the prettiest little baby doll. She was smaller than Lucille, but she sure was beautiful. Her head and body were made of muslin. Her dress was blue and white gingham with three tiny pearly-white buttons fastening it together in the front. Yellow yarn hung down long and straight around her head like locks of golden hair. Soft blue eyes and a pink smile were carefully stitched on her face.

I couldn't believe my eyes. "Rae, she's beautiful."

"And she's yours, Dahlia. Now you have your own Lucille. Only I was thinking maybe you'd like to call her Daisy because of her sunshiny hair."

"I was just thinking I might name her Rae," I said.

Rae blushed. "Maybe you could put those

together and call her Daisy Rae."

And that's just what I did.

VI

The rest of that summer I carried Daisy Rae everywhere with me. She slept with me at night. She sat in my lap at the breakfast table. And I kept her squeezed under my arm if Mommy sent me out to gather eggs.

Mr. Walker had a little chicken coop about fifteen steps from the side of that unpainted house. Our chickens had roosted in the trees back up on the mountain, so this was a fine set-up. He gave Mommy nearly a dozen hens and a rooster to start off, since she had to leave her chickens behind. Those hens were not very friendly, and that rooster pranced around on his pointy little claws like he owned the place.

I usually tried to hide when Mommy needed somebody to gather the eggs. Celia could walk right up to a nesting box and lift a hen with one hand while she snatched an egg with the other. Not me. I'd try my best to sneak up on those chickens, but they always caught me. When they squawked and flapped and pecked at my hands, I jumped like the dickens. One time I dropped a whole pail of eggs and every one of them busted.

Gathering eggs was not for me. I didn't mind churning butter. But to churn butter, we needed our cow, and it wasn't until near the end of that first summer that we had her.

Mr. Walker and Poppy made a trip back up to the mountain in the huckster truck. Right away, Charlie asked to go with them, but Poppy said he had to stay back and mind the farm. But I didn't see any reason why I couldn't go.

"Please, Poppy, please!" I begged. "I want to show Daisy Rae Zeke's cabin and the creek and the flat rock and Grandpap!" I hadn't forgotten about that treasure, either. I figured maybe Daisy Rae could be my good luck charm and we just might find it.

Mommy was the one who answered. "This is not a pleasure trip, child. I'm just a-hopin' they'll make it back here safe with Ol' Rosie." Her eyes looked a little bit sad and so far off.

"Can he at least bring Grandpap back with him?" I asked. "I want him to meet Daisy Rae."

Mommy sighed. "He might be a little harder to move than a cow," she said. Then she patted my head and walked away.

Ol' Rosie was quite a burden if you ask my opinion. Back on the mountain, early in the morning, before she made breakfast, Mommy had to march out to the shed to milk Ol' Rosie. She'd let that cow graze in the pasture until late afternoon. Then Mommy had to tread across the long shadows and tall grass, pull Ol' Rosie back to the shed, and milk her all over again. You'd think she'd be happy to be rid of that burden.

When I told Ruby I wanted to go back up home for a visit, she put her hands on her hips and looked like she was scolding me. "Now, Dahlia Harrell," she said, "you know that school will be starting in just a few short weeks. You need to set your mind on getting ready."

Ruby's excitement about school made me nervous. Last year I got sick, so I still hadn't made it all the way through the second grade. What if I couldn't remember anything I'd learned? Charlie, Rae, and Celia had gone to school when they could, but it was a long walk, and if the weather was bad, Mommy didn't feel safe about them going off. Then we up and moved to Lothian Mill, and we'd been too busy to even think about school.

"You need some new dresses and a new pair of shoes–" Ruby stopped suddenly. Maybe she realized I'd never had a store-bought dress in my life. Maybe she noticed I was wearing a hand-me-down dress Mommy made from a flour sack. What she was thinking, I'll never know. She changed the subject and didn't mention it to me again.

Ruby must've mentioned it to her Momma though, because soon after that, Miss Bessie showed up with a tape measure. She stretched it out on the floor, and we all took turns stepping on it with our bare feet. I'd been without shoes all summer, so I was a little bit ashamed to have all that attention put on my dirty feet. But Miss Bessie didn't seem to mind. She just wrote down numbers and chattered away.

"Now Mary, don't you fret," she told Mommy. "Rev. Shumate and the Ladies' Relief Society want to see to it that you all have what you need for a good start to the school year." Miss Bessie was a member of the Ladies' Relief Society, and I think she made us their special project.

Not long after the foot-measuring day, some women from the Lothian Mill church drove up to the unpainted house and unloaded all kinds of nice things. There were two pairs of shoes for each of us. My school shoes were black ankle boots with buttonholes and a hook for pulling the buttons through each little hole. There were also white shoes with a buckle on each side. Miss Bessie said, "These will be your Sunday church shoes."

From the corner of my eye, I saw Mommy look down at the floor right away. Miss Bessie had invited us to the Lothian Mill Church several times, but Poppy kept making excuses. Last time she asked, he said his children didn't have proper shoes to wear to church. Miss Bessie went and fixed that.

Rae got some white church shoes with a little bit of a heel on the back and a t-strap across the top. They had a fancy silver buckle on the side, and they made a *clop-clop* sound as she walked across the wood floor. Her school shoes were black and had flat bottoms. They didn't come up on the ankle like mine, and they had one big button on the side instead of a bunch of little ones.

Celia's school shoes were just like Rae's, but her church shoes were like mine. I could see her eyeing Rae's heels with a jealous mind. But she couldn't complain, because she got the prettiest dresses out of all of us.

We got four or five dresses apiece – some for school and some for church. My favorite dress was navy blue with a round white color and puff sleeves. There was a pale pink one for me to wear to church. It had a lace trim around the bottom of it. I just stood there in my faded flour-sack dress and hugged those new clothes. It hadn't even occurred to me yet to be ashamed for getting all that charity.

Celia went and put on a beautiful new dress right away and started dancing around in circles. It was white with a long straight skirt and a lace collar. She looked almost like an angel, even if she didn't act like one.

"Now I expect that you will not put a hand on my new dresses, Dahlia," she warned. "Especially this white one." She swayed side to side and watched the fabric flow like waves of water. "It's just perfect, and I don't want to see any dirty little fingerprints soiling it."

I wanted to grab ahold and mess it up as soon as she said that, but the ladies from the Relief Society smiled and walked right between us.

Charlie crept into the room just a little ways. He stared at the floor, his hands stuffed in the pockets of his faded brown pants and dirty ankles sticking out from under the frayed hems.

One of the ladies walked toward him carrying a stack of pants, shirts, and overalls folded neatly and tied with brown twine. A pair of brown boots with only a few scuffs crowned the top of the stack.

Another lady followed, her warm smile reflecting off shiny black shoes. Charlie kept his head bowed. He sort of nodded at the ladies as he took the clothes and shoes. Then he turned around without saying a word and walked up the stairs to his attic room.

Mommy watched him, and I couldn't help but think she looked smaller than usual, standing there next to those nice women. She said a real kind thank you to the Ladies' Relief Society, but it looked like tears were welling up in her eyes. I sure didn't feel like crying. That day was better than any Christmas we'd ever had.

Before leaving, those ladies brought a heap of food into our kitchen. There was salty country ham, apples, plum jelly, cornbread, apple cider, and a cherry pie. "Well, this is a day to remember!" Miss Bessie said as she waved the ladies off in their car. Then she walked back up to her big white house, humming a happy tune.

Soon after that day of gifts, Mr. Walker and Poppy came back from the mountain. I was gently rocking back and forth on the beech tree swing all by myself when a cloud of dust carried the huckster truck up the dirt road toward the barn. I climbed up on the porch, straining to see through the haze.

Mr. Walker parked under a shady crabapple tree, and when the dust settled, I spotted Ol' Rosie tied up in the back. I'm sure she didn't know what to think. Mommy let the screen door slam as she ran out of the house. She rubbed her hands on her apron, and then she waved them in the air. I couldn't believe my eyes, but she actually jumped up in the truck bed and hugged that cow!

While Mommy welcomed Ol' Rosie to Mr. Walker's farm, I worked my way to the front seat. I stepped up on the running board and looked inside, hoping I might find Grandpap. But Poppy sat there all alone, resting in the shade of the crabapple tree.

Finally, Poppy climbed out and stretched after the long ride. He patted my head and whispered, "He just can't bear to leave that mountain, Dahlia." And the shadow between us felt as heavy as a five-gallon keg of water.

While everyone gathered outside, laughing, hugging, and tugging at Ol' Rosie, I ran into the parlor where I'd left Daisy Rae. I poured out tears and told her she wouldn't meet Grandpap after all. I told her how much he would have liked her blue eyes, soft smile, and pure, loving heart. I also promised her that when we finally dug up that treasure, I'd never replace her with a store-bought doll.

Celia heard me crying, and she pounced like a barn cat on a mouse. "You are such a baby! You're in here crying while the rest of us are working! Somebody has to help get that cow in the barn. Then the cow needs settlin', supper needs fixin', and there are about a thousand other things that need to be done. But here you are, crying like a little baby and talkin' to a rag doll!"

Celia stomped off in her own cloud of dust, and I felt meanness well up inside me like a sudden thunderstorm. I hurried up to our room and found her white angel dress lying across the foot of the bed. I set Daisy Rae down carefully on the chest of drawers and climbed up on the bed. Then I took my dirty bare feet and stomped on that dress a bunch of times.

When I felt satisfied, I got down off the bed, moved that dress under the others, and raced outside. Rae was trying to get the chickens in their pens while everyone else seemed to be in the barn. I told her I would tend to the chickens.

"That's a good idea, Dahlia. Mommy's still trying to get Ol' Rosie milked and settled. Celia's helping her. Mr. Walker needs Poppy and Charlie to help him tend to a few things. I think I'd better start on supper."

Rae looked tired but calm as she climbed up the steps and into the house. I didn't feel like crying anymore. I plopped down on the ground and listened to the chickens chatter. The sun sank down behind the far-off mountains, and darkness crept in a little at a time.

VII

That night, I sat through supper all twisted up in knots. Part of me was still so mad at Celia that I was glad about what I'd done. The rest of me was just plain scared because I knew there would be a price to pay when she discovered the dirty smudges on her new white dress.

Lucky for me, it was dark by the time we finished eating. Rae and Mommy went out to check on Ol' Rosie while Celia and I cleared the table. Charlie heated some water for washing dishes, and Poppy said he needed to stretch out and rest his eyes.

Celia never said a word to me as we worked. I scraped dishes over the slop bucket while she paraded back and forth across the kitchen putting things in their places. Her mouth was drawn up tight like a buttonhole. Her dark hair was a mess, and the fingernails she always filed and kept so clean had dirt wedged under them. I almost felt sorry for her.

When Mommy came back in the kitchen, she washed the dishes while we silently dried and put them away. A couple of times she began to hum a tune, but she gave out pretty quick. Mommy's face looked content, but she kept leaning forward, and every time she had one hand loose, she would hold it on her back like she was trying to keep herself from falling over.

We finally trudged upstairs, and we tiptoed around to get into nightclothes because Rae was already sound asleep. She had scooped up all the dresses and laid them in a pile over the back of the wooden chair in the corner. They were nothing but a big gray lump when we crawled in the bed.

Celia was out almost as soon as her head hit the pillow. I was having a hard time finding sleep. That big gray lump took on frightening shapes. First it was a monster, and then a ghost, and finally it was Celia, crouching down ready to spring at me and tear me to shreds.

Our preacher back home said if you had faith the size of a mustard seed, you could move a mountain. I didn't need to move a mountain, but I sure did need those smudges to disappear from Celia's dress.

I squeezed my eyes shut and prayed in my head

so I was sure Celia wouldn't hear me. *Dear God, I know you can wash away the stains from that dress and make it white as snow, so I'm asking you to please go ahead and do that. Amen.*

The next couple of days were busy ones, and no one had time to fool with the dresses. Mommy had a lot of trouble getting Ol' Rosie to stand still and give her milk. Maybe it was the dusty ride to a new barn, or maybe Grandpap hadn't kept up with the milking, or maybe she was just being ornery. All we knew was that Mommy was spending a lot of time in the barn and we weren't getting much milk.

When Saturday rolled around, it was time for baths. Poppy told us to wash up extra clean and shiny because the next day we were all going to the Lothian Mill Church. Since the Rev. Shumate and all those women from the Ladies' Relief Society had been so generous with us, Poppy said we had to go. Mommy looked a little nervous and told us to be sure to wear the pretty church dresses and shiny church shoes.

My insides were a twisted mess. Mommy put her hand on my shoulder and said, "I know the Lothian Mill Church is going to be different, and there might be a bunch of people we don't know, but we'll be just fine." I wasn't sure if she was talking to me or to herself.

I was the first one ready Sunday morning. I jumped into my dress and shoes and pushed my hair back out of my face with my hands. Celia and Rae were still in their nightclothes working on each other's hair. Celia smelled like she spilled rose water all over herself. I heard Mommy in the kitchen, so I thought I'd go make myself useful.

"My, my, you sure do look nice!" Mommy was pulling biscuits from the oven with one hand and stirring gravy with the other. She had her apron tied around her white church dress.

I smiled and tilted my head to one side, trying to live up to my nice-looking outfit. "Is there anything I can do to help?"

"Put some butter and jam on the table, and then come stir this gravy while I get the biscuits squared away."

I sashayed back and forth across the kitchen, swinging my hips so that the lace trim on my dress tickled the sides of my legs as it flowed back and forth. Once I got the butter and jam set up, I sashayed back to the stove and took the long wooden spoon from Mommy's hands. She immediately shuffled the biscuits into her long wooden bread bowl, covered them with a towel, and then turned to cool the oven. All the while, I stirred and stirred that gravy, trying to stir away the little quivers that kept sneaking up on me.

Suddenly, Mommy let the oven door slam shut and it startled me. The spoon flipped up out of the pot and splattered hot gravy on her face, in her hair, and all down the front of her apron.

"Lord, child, I don't know whether you help or hinder!" Right away, she grabbed the towel off the top of the biscuits and rubbed her face. She pulled her apron off and started fussing with the front of her dress. "I'll finish up in here. You go run a brush through that hair and tell your sisters to hurry up."

Going back into that room was the last thing I wanted to do. I decided it would be best to just walk in, grab my hairbrush, pull one stroke through each side, and hurry back out. But just as I reached for the brush, Celia picked up her dress. She took one look at those black footprints and flipped back toward me like a swinging door.

She snatched the hairbrush out of my hand and reared back like she was going to hit me with it. Somewhere in that blurry moment I heard her yell, "You wicked baby!"

Rae jumped in and caught Celia's arm just before the brush reached my nose. "Celia, what are you doing?" she shouted.

Celia screeched like a wild animal. "Why do you have to ruin everything, Dahlia? Why?!"

By that time, Poppy appeared in our room wearing an angry scowl with his one good suit. "What's going on in here?" he hollered.

"Dahlia ruined my new dress, Poppy!" Celia held it up so he could see the smudges.

Then Rae calmly asked what I thought was a very good question. "Celia, how do you know Dahlia did something to your dress?" Poppy raised his eyebrows and Rae continued. "Dahlia just walked back into the room. I could have easily dropped it when I was putting it over on that wooden chair."

Celia thought for a minute. "Did you?" she asked Rae.

"No, not that I recall," Rae said, "but I was so tired when I moved those dresses. I could have done just about anything that night and not remember it now."

At that point, I knew I should go ahead and tell the truth. It was the right thing to do. But at that moment I was less concerned with right and wrong, and more concerned with saving my hide.

"We'll get it cleaned up, Celia," Poppy offered.

"By the time your mommy gets finished, it'll look like it has a fresh coat of whitewash." His voice sounded less angry but a little impatient.

Celia didn't smile, but her breathing slowed down and her shoulders caved in a little.

"Just wear one of those other dresses for now, and we'll take care of it tomorrow," Poppy said. "Now, hurry up. I'll be a-waiting downstairs."

I grabbed Daisy Rae, scurried out the door, and followed him to the kitchen. Mommy and Charlie were already seated, so we joined them. Soon enough, my sisters arrived. Celia had decided to wear a black dress that had a real straight skirt to it. The hem came to rest just above her ankles. There was a rounded white collar at the top, but other than that, it was all black. We ate our bite of breakfast and then rushed outside to meet up with Ruby's family.

We strolled along behind the Walkers all the way to the church with two red doors on the front. The men all went in the left door, and the women went in the right. Poppy and Charlie sat with the men. The rest of us filled up one short pew on the women's side of the church.

I followed Mommy and squeezed up next to her. Rae slid in by me, straightening her pretty pink dress over her legs and greeting the people around us with a bright smile.

Finally, along came Celia, strolling quietly down the aisle, dressed for a funeral. All the sunlight streaming through the long narrow windows and all the light-of-the-world preaching we heard were not powerful enough to remove the darkness from her that morning.

VIII

The further it got into summer, the more Miss Bessie and Ruby talked about school. And the more they talked about it, the more Mommy fretted over it. "I reckon I should've gotten them signed up for the Lothian Mill School back in the spring. We were just so busy a-gettin' settled and there was so much work that needed doing."

"Not to worry, Mary," Miss Bessie told her. "We have a couple of fine teachers and they'll get the children caught up in no time at all."

Miss Bessie went with us up to the schoolhouse to help Mommy fill out some papers. The Lothian Mill School was set back off the road down past the church. It was made of whitewashed wood slats and had a set of unpainted wood steps leading up to a thick brown door.

We followed Miss Bessie right through that door and up to a desk where a skinny, dark-haired lady looked at us over the top of little wiry eyeglasses. She didn't smile, and she mostly just talked to Miss Bessie as if Mommy wasn't even there.

I had pictured rows of chairs and slates, but we were in a small room that was some kind of entryway. There were long benches, like church pews, along the side walls. A set of shelves sat behind the dark-haired lady. It was stacked tight with books and papers, and on each side of the shelves there was a door.

After the lady handed over a stack of papers, we sat down on a long wooden bench and listened to Miss Bessie read a bunch of questions out loud. She tried to be quiet, but her whispers echoed off the ceiling and walls. Mommy talked through the answers while Miss Bessie did all the writing.

I knew Mommy could read and write a bit because she read from the Bible to us sometimes, and she used to sign our notes at Pete Gaddy's store when we needed to use credit. Poppy only knew how to put an X for his name, which is what a lot of folks up on the mountain did. I don't know how Pete Gaddy kept it all straight.

I was halfway playing with Daisy Rae and halfway eavesdropping as Mommy answered Miss Bessie's questions. "Charlie's fourteen, but he's missed a lot of school. Sometimes John needed him to stay and help with the farm. Then there was a time when he broke his leg. He missed several months of school." Her voice trailed off. I remembered hearing Charlie say he didn't even want to go to school, but Mommy told him it was important.

Miss Bessie nodded as she wrote some things down on the paper. Then she said, "Let's move on to Rae."

"Rae's twelve years old, and she's always done real good in school." Mommy smiled. Rae always tried to please everybody, no matter where she was. She practiced her writing all the time, with a stick in the dirt, with her sewing and embroidery, and on paper when she had some. Rae was the only one excited about getting back to school.

I leaned in when Miss Bessie asked about Celia, but Mommy didn't say much. "Celia's ten, and she's got pretty handwriting. I know she should be farther along, but she's only finished through the third grade so far." Miss Bessie nodded and scribbled on the paper.

I was listening extra hard when they got to me. "Dahlia got off to a late start, like Celia. And then she missed a fair portion of the second grade on account of diphtheria." She leaned over close to Miss Bessie and added, "Dahlia didn't take to school so well in the first place." I felt a fever rise up in my face and I had to fight like the dickens to keep the tears from falling.

Miss Bessie patted Mommy's hand. "It's all right, Mary," she said. "I'm sure Dahlia will catch up quickly. Ruby's just now starting in the second grade. They can work together." I felt a little hollowed out at the thought of starting second grade all over again, but working with Ruby took the sting away. Then Miss Bessie stood up and said, "Believe me, Dahlia will learn so much from Miss Mattie Coombs."

Miss Mattie Coombs. That was the first time I heard my teacher's name. I imagined a round, friendly mother-type person like Miss Bessie. I imagined that she would dote over Ruby and me, and that she would give Daisy Rae her own seat in the class. I imagined that I would come home reading big books and writing my own stories after the first day of school. All those things I had imagined were wrong, but I was not disappointed with Miss Mattie Coombs.

On the first day of school, Mommy walked us to the main road where we met up with Miss Bessie, Ruby, and the boys. Mommy and Miss Bessie only walked a short piece, and then they stopped and waved us on. Dwight Jr. led the way to the schoolhouse. He kept talking to Charlie like he was trying to drag him along with a string of words.

Wayne and Hoyt shuffled behind them, pushing and shoving each other every few steps. Rae and Celia walked side by side, followed by Ruby and me. Most of the way, Ruby chattered on like a hen. She had already been attending the Lothian Mill School for a year, so she knew all about it.

"The schoolhouse is divided into two classrooms – the left side is for grades one through four, and the right side is for grades five through eight." That was different from the mountain school. It went up to the eighth grade too, but it was just a one-room schoolhouse full of benches.

"The teacher for the higher grades is Miss Eunice Dill," Ruby told me. Then she leaned over and whispered, "She's old and wrinkly and mean as a snake!" I already felt scared for Charlie and Rae.

"You are just gonna love Miss Mattie Coombs," Ruby continued. "She's just the opposite. She's young and kind and beautiful like a flower!" While Ruby kept chattering, I silently mouthed *Miss Coombs* over and over again, trying to make it feel natural to my lips.

The others had gotten ahead of us, and we were taking giant steps to catch up. With every step, I heard coins jingle in Ruby's pocket. "Did you bring snack money?" she asked.

I kept looking forward as we walked. "I have my lunch pail. Mommy wrapped up a couple of biscuits and some ham, and I have a tomato from her garden."

Ruby froze in her tracks and put her hands on her hips. "First of all, how are you going to eat a whole tomato? I've only ever had tomato sliced up. And second of all," she was walking again, "the ladies from the church sell the cutest little bottles of milk at lunch time. Then they'll come back again with an afternoon snack. It's usually fruit, but every once in a while they have oatmeal cookies."

"First of all," I answered, trying to imitate her voice and sound like I wasn't bothered at all, "I like eating whole tomatoes. I bite into them just like apples. But they're better than apples because you don't have to work your way around a core." The words flowed from my mouth, but my mind was stuck on the snack money.

"Second of all," I said, "I think I'll be kind of full after my lunch. I don't think I'll be wanting anything in the afternoon." That was an outright lie, but I was determined to make it seem like the truth.

By that time we had caught up to the others, and

I noticed that Ruby's brothers had a jingle in their pockets, too. The school up on the mountain never sold milk or snacks. I wondered if Charlie, Rae, and Celia knew about this discouraging fact. There was no way we'd ever have extra change jingling in our pockets.

When we finally made it to the schoolhouse, there were a few boys chasing each other around the yard and a group of girls sitting on the steps. We had to weave through them to get to the big brown door.

Inside, we found that skinny lady with wiry glasses. She was sitting at her desk with a neat stack of papers in front of her and a sharp pencil in her hand. She still wasn't smiling.

Once she checked for our names on her pieces of paper, she pointed toward the door we needed to go through. Ruby, Celia, and I went to the left. Charlie, Rae, and all of Ruby's brothers went to the right. I felt a little quivery inside when we split up, but Ruby grabbed my hand and squeezed it.

"I am so excited!" she whispered in my ear.

The moment we stepped onto that creaky classroom floor, a slender hand reached out to greet us. Right away, Ruby shook the hand like she was a grown-up and said, "Good morning, Miss Coombs."

Then she said, "This is Dahlia. She's new here."

The slender hand was reaching out toward me, and I just stared at it. I wasn't sure if I was supposed to say something or not. "I'm Miss Coombs," said the voice behind the hand, "and I will be your teacher."

The voice was kind and gentle, like I'd imagined. It belonged to a pale, thin woman with soft brown hair that curled in tiny ringlets around her face. The rest of her hair was twisted up and pinned tight on the back of her head. She had copper-colored eyes and a warm smile.

Ruby nudged me. "Shake her hand!"

As soon as I reached out, Miss Coombs wrapped both of her hands around mine and closed her lips in a softer smile. "Welcome, Dahlia," she said, and then she pointed us toward our desks.

Right about that time a bell rang. More children tramped into the classroom, and Miss Coombs showed them to their desks. Actually, they were chairs with tabletops sticking off the back for the person behind to write on. They all had little cut-out circles for inkwells, but only some desks *had* inkwells. The rest of us had slates and chalk sticks.

Ruby sat beside me, and right away, she started writing. Her letters were neat and straight, and I winced thinking about the chalk and slate Miss Bessie had given me for practicing. They were tucked under the bed upstairs, still clean and new.

The girl in front of Ruby swirled around and smiled. "Hi, my name is Rosie." Rosie had white-blond hair tied up with a long red ribbon like the one Celia used to have. Blue ruffles spilled out all around her, and her slate was full of words.

Ruby whispered back her own name and added, "This is Dahlia." Rosie looked at me for a long moment but didn't say anything. My face felt warm and my insides were full of that bee-buzzing feeling. I looked away.

My eyes found Celia across the room in her ink well desk. She straightened her skirt and sat prim and proper, trying to be so serious. The girl in front of her turned around and smiled. Celia just ignored her.

In the corner beyond Celia there was a wood-burning stove, and across the front, a blackboard stretched almost from one wall to the other. It held lots of words, but I couldn't make out what they said.

A pretty shade tree stood outside the window to my left. It looked like a picture in a frame, and in the background of the picture was a graveyard. I was trying to count all the headstones when Miss Coombs suddenly stepped in and blocked my view.

"Dahlia, did you read my directions?" She wasn't smiling anymore. "Please write a paragraph to introduce yourself."

I swallowed hard as the chalk trembled in my hand, but I couldn't think fast enough to come up with words. And a paragraph? I'd never written a paragraph in my entire life.

Miss Coombs leaned down and spoke quietly. "Are you able to write a sentence?"

Suddenly, the floor fell out from under me. I was on that beech tree swing again, sailing way up over the rooftop. I tried to stop them, but tears fell from my eyes like silent raindrops.

"There is no sense in crying." Miss Coombs brought a book to my desk and pointed at a page. "Can you read this sentence to me?"

Words floated on the page and smeared into a blur of black and white. I shook my head and realized eyes were fixed on me from every direction. Again, my face burned and I fought the tears that strained to fall and the feet that screamed to run out of the schoolhouse, across the many winding roads, and back to the mountain. Back to Grandpap and peaches and dahlias and a maybe-treasure that could change me into a girl with ribbons and ruffles and words all over her slate.

"Well, I think I know where we need to begin," Miss Coombs said matter-of-factly. "Class, return to your work, please. I'll be watching for a qualified assistant to help distribute your McGuffey Readers."

Everyone went back to work, and Miss Coombs brought a different book to my desk. "This is a primer," she said. "It will help you learn the words you'll need for making sense of stories and writing sentences." She pointed out letters and asked me about their sounds.

Suddenly, it was coming back to me. Miss Coombs let out a big breath. "Let's try these words." She sounded out the words, letter by letter, and I repeated:

"Kuh – a – tuh. A cat. Ruh – a – tuh. A rat."

"That's fine, now," Miss Coombs said. Then she turned the page. "Work on using those sounds to read these words and simple sentences. I'll be back to check on you soon."

All morning, I plugged along sounding out words while Miss Coombs rushed about from student to student. She began rearranging students. She moved me next to a quiet girl with matted hair. Her name was Ida, and she wore a flour sack dress like the one I wore when the Ladies' Relief Society came to visit.

Ida wasn't even sure of all the letters and sounds, so it was slow going getting her to say the words. Miss Coombs kept wandering back to listen to us. She made us repeat the words and sentences over and over until we read them smoothly.

Nat. Hat. Fan. Can.
Ann and Nat.
Ann has a fan.
Nat has a hat.
Ann can fan Nat.

I'd finally had about enough of that, and I was eyeing my empty seat by Ruby. I was thinking it must be about time for us to move back to our real seats. Then Ida went and interrupted my thinking. "I like your dress."

"Thanks," I said, to be polite. I knew it would also be polite to say a compliment back to her, but that old flour sack dress was faded and dirty. Her shoes were way too small, and somebody had cut the fronts of them off so her toes could come out. Ida's hair was a tangled mess and her fingernails were black. I couldn't think of anything to say.

Right then, Miss Coombs' voice rattled my thoughts. "Rosie, please move back to this seat." I turned and saw her point to *my* desk next to Ruby.

That white-haired girl stood up and said, "Yes, ma'am." Then Ruby smiled like she was actually excited, and I felt a fiery pain in my chest. The only thing that kept me from crying was knowing that girl had the same name as Mommy's cow.

"Do you wanna go back to the first page and start a-readin' the letters and sounds again?" Ida asked.

I thought, *No, I don't. If we keep starting over, I'll never catch up to where Ruby is and I'll be stuck here with you forever.* I thought that, but I didn't say it. Instead, I turned the book back and we started again.

As I listened to Ida struggle to match letters to sounds, I kept looking over my shoulder at Ruby. She never looked back at me. She and that Rosie girl had their heads buried in those McGuffey Readers. Miss Coombs smiled at them every time she passed.

Whenever she looked my way, she either said, "That's it, Ida, keep starting over until you can move smoothly," or "Dahlia, pay attention to your work."

By lunchtime, I was plenty hungry and ready to talk with Ruby. I followed her out to a shady spot in the schoolyard, but then Rosie joined us too. They kept bursting into giggles, but I didn't understand what was so funny.

While I was trying to think of something clever to say, Ida's shadow crept up on me from behind. I hoped if I ignored her she'd go away. But then Rosie said, "Dahlia, I think your friend would like to sit with you." I scooted over, feeling very irritated, and let Ida squeeze into our little circle.

Ida didn't say a word all of lunchtime. She just nibbled on a dry biscuit, the only thing in her lunch pail. I knew I should ask if she wanted a piece of ham, but I was hungry and the thought of sharing with her did not appeal to me.

Suddenly, Rosie jumped up all excited and said, "Look!" Two ladies were coming out of the church, rolling a cart full of little glass milk bottles. Children lined up to spend two cents apiece buying milk. Some of them even bought two bottles!

The ladies wore smiles on their faces and hats on their heads. The lady in the gray hat said, "Now, we'll have some oatmeal cookies after school, so be sure to save a penny for a cookie!" Ruby and Rosie started giggling again, and they jumped up and down in circles, coins jingling in their pockets.

I looked across the schoolyard and saw Rae sitting in the grass with a group of girls. They talked and smiled, seeming unaware of the ladies in hats. Charlie leaned up against a tree all alone, and Celia was on the steps with those same girls we had to weave around that morning.

Just as the milk bottle business seemed to be settling down, the lady in the gray hat sang out, "Listen for your last name, children. If you hear me call it, you come on over to the cart." Ida's last name was Buck, and that was the first name called. Ida stood up nervously and straightened out her flour sack dress. She took little steps toward the cart with her head bowed down the whole time.

I was so curious watching her that I almost didn't hear the gray-hat lady say, "Harrell!" I hurried to catch up with Ida. Charlie, Rae, and Celia all walked cautiously toward the cart with squinted eyes and puzzled frowns.

By the time they stopped calling names, seventeen of us were gathered at the milk cart, all looking sad and pitiful for some reason. The gray-hat lady explained, "You children will be allowed to have the leftover milk each day for free, starting with the youngest."

Ida and I took our little glass milk bottles from the hands of the silent lady – the one in the black hat – and we were silent right back at her. As we walked past the others, I saw that Celia and Charlie had wrinkled their faces into angry frowns, but they took the milk anyway. Of course, I heard Rae politely say she'd prefer to let someone else have her milk.

After lunch, we had some recess time in the schoolyard. I dodged the balls being kicked and thrown, and headed toward some girls playing hopscotch in the dirt. Ruby popped up and surprised me. She grabbed my hand and dragged me over to some jump ropes. "Let me show you some tricks!" she squealed.

Rosie was on one end of a long rope, and a girl named Florence was on the other. They turned the rope and Ruby hopped right in. She jumped up and down a bunch of times, turned back and forth, and even touched the ground before she hopped back out.

Then it was my turn. I watched the rope come around and around. Each time I thought I'd jump in, an invisible wall seemed to hold me back. Finally, Florence let out a really loud sigh to let me know I was wearing out her patience. So I closed my eyes and jumped.

I hopped up and down just like Ruby did, but instead of jumping over the rope, I jumped on top of it with one foot, and then sprang off it so fast that it came around and slapped me on the opposite leg.

"Your turn's up," Florence said, sighing again. I strolled slowly to the end of the line. Standing there in half-sun and half-shadow, I tried to ignore my stinging leg and hoped that recess would soon be over.

The afternoon was filled with arithmetic, which seemed to me to be a little easier than words and sentences. Writing numbers neatly was something I would have to practice, but at least I could figure out how to count them up, add them together, and take them away pretty easily.

Just before time to go home, Miss Coombs read to the whole class from a book called *The Secret Garden*. It was about a spoiled girl who had servants taking care of her. Her parents died, but it was hard to feel sorry for her because she was so mean and disagreeable. And because she had fancy clothes and all those servants. Her name was Mary, just like Mommy, but that was the only thing alike about them.

Finally, the school bell rang and we filed back out to the school yard for our long walk home. The hat ladies were selling their oatmeal cookies, and Ruby ran straight to their cart. I walked right past her, staring at the dusty ground and wishing we had never left Zeke's cabin. My feet followed the long shadows of my sisters and brother. They didn't say it, but I think they were wishing the same thing.

IX

The leaves changed color, the days got shorter, and the cool winds came to call. And all the while, Miss Coombs kept reading to us from *The Secret Garden*. That was my favorite part of each day. Mean little Mary got to go and live with her rich uncle, Master Craven. He might've been related to the Rockefellers because he had a big, fancy house called Misselthwaite Manor.

Master Craven was never home, though. He was off traveling most of the time because his wife had died and he was so lonesome without her. A strict lady named Mrs. Medlock was in charge of the house. (I pictured her looking a lot like Miss Eunice Dill, the upper grade teacher.) Mary made friends with a servant girl named Martha, but Martha came from a poor family and she had to work for Mary, so I don't know if you could really call them friends.

Mean little Mary snooped around and uncovered a bunch of secrets. She found an old overgrown garden and decided to fix it up. She learned that Martha had a brother named Dickon who was real good with plants and animals, so she got him to help with the garden. Her biggest discovery was Colin, Master Craven's son. He stayed hidden away in his room because he was sick all the time.

The garden had belonged to Colin's mother. It was her favorite place, but it was also the place where she died. She had climbed up in a tree to read a book, and the branch she was sitting on broke. She fell to the ground so hard it killed her. But that happened way before the story started.

I liked it when Miss Coombs read to us, mostly because I liked the story, but partly because it meant our schoolwork was done for the day. Until I went to the Lothian Mill School, I never knew you could work so hard while you were sitting still. I had to write and read all kinds of words, and do a bunch of figuring with numbers. Every time I thought I was finished, Miss Coombs would get me started all over again.

I liked arithmetic. It came to me a lot easier than the reading. You could rely on numbers to act the same way all the time, but letters were always tricking you and making different sounds. Whenever I felt discouraged though, I had to remind myself that at least I wasn't having as hard a time as poor Ida. Sometimes Miss Coombs would ask me to be her helper.

For the first month or so of school, Ruby had been my helper. When we walked to and from school, she quizzed me on number problems and spelling words. But when we got home in the afternoons, Miss Bessie insisted that Ruby go in the house, eat a snack, and do her homework. If she didn't have any homework, Miss Bessie made Ruby read to her from one of the books they had on a shelf in their parlor.

We didn't have any books in our house, except for the Bible. Sometimes Mommy would read to us from the Bible, or sometimes she would ask Charlie or Rae to do it. Rae always seemed to like to read out loud, but Mommy had to make Charlie do it.

When we came home, there was always work to be done. Charlie had to change out of his school clothes right away and head out to the fields to help Poppy. The rest of us knew there'd be a list of chores waiting for us.

Mommy was always working. She scrubbed clothes on a washboard, sewed, mended, tended her kitchen garden, cooked, and of course, milked that cow every morning and every evening. You never found her sitting idle. Even if she sat out on the front porch, she'd carry some mending in her hands or have her apron pulled up to hold a mess of beans that needed snapping.

We couldn't let Mommy catch us being idle. She could come up with a list of chores faster than Charlie could swing a hammer. *Take those dry things down from the line. Go and hang these wet clothes on the line. Run and fill this basket with berries. Go out and collect some eggs. There's butter to be churned. Stir those beans before they burn to the pot. I need someone to pull these weeds. Child, grab that broom and sweep the dirt out of this house before it puts down roots.*

With schoolwork, homework, and Mommy's never-ending chore list, I didn't have much time for playing. All the while, Rosie cozied up to Ruby. She even walked home with Ruby and ate supper at the Walkers' house. That's something we hadn't done since our very first night in Lothian Mill.

My stomach carried a little knot ever since the start of school, and it festered and grew whenever I thought about Ruby. She used to come around nearly every day, but that ended with the summer. I hung onto our long walks to and from school. It was the only time I could really count on Ruby being there.

One crisp October Friday, we walked home

through a rainbow of swirling colors. Ruby and I stomped on dry brown leaves along the dirt road just to hear them crunch. The gently moving air carried a feeling of change, and the whole world was pleasant.

"It's Friday!" Ruby shouted into the cool, blue afternoon. "No homework! No school tomorrow! I just want to play!"

"I just want to play!" I repeated, throwing my arms out to mimic her.

Ruby leaned in close and whispered, "Do you want me to ask my Momma if I can come down to your house and play until suppertime?"

Without even thinking about asking Mommy I said, "Yes!"

"I just need to change my clothes, eat a snack, and do my reading," she said, still keeping her voice low. "Then I'll grab Lucille and come to your house. I'm sure Momma will say it's fine." Ruby's eyes lit up with excitement and she squealed.

That's when Celia stopped and cut her squinty, dark eyes toward us. "I don't know what you're whispering about, but you can be thankful you're still a carefree child," she snapped. "I have a book report due Monday, and I haven't even read the book yet. As soon as I get home I have to start reading, and I'll be working on it all weekend."

I was trying to figure out what that had to do with me when Rae said, "Well, Celia, maybe you shouldn't put things off."

Celia swung around with fire in those dark eyes. "Maybe if I could find a minute of peace and quiet when nobody's yellin' or singin' or tellin' me to feed chickens or wash dishes, I wouldn't be in this fix!"

Rae hurried to catch up with Charlie and the boys, and Celia stomped on alone, shattering leaves and kicking up dirt.

I hung back and put a good bit of distance between Celia and me. Ruby stayed by my side. When she knew Celia wasn't looking, Ruby rolled her eyes and twirled a finger in circles up by her head, saying Celia was crazy. Then she doubled over laughing. I laughed along with her, but something dark and heavy tugged at me on the inside.

Ruby could already read as well as Celia – maybe better! Of course, she had shelves lined with books, and Miss Bessie sat there and listened to her read every afternoon. Ruby never had to feed chickens or tend to any farm work. Her daddy hired people for that.

Suddenly, it occurred to me that as soon as I got

home, Mommy would rattle off a list of things that needed to be done. I sure enough had to find a way to wriggle out of her chores and slip outside.

"I'll meet you out by the back door," I told Ruby. "Don't bother coming up to the front porch." Ruby tilted her head and scrunched her face up like she was going to ask why, but I didn't give her time. "That way we'll be closer to the apple orchard. We can pretend it's *The Secret Garden*!" Ruby loved that book, so she gasped with delight.

The apple orchard was out behind the fields. Thick rows of trees were filling up with fruit. Poppy and Charlie had been out there a lot lately gathering apples. Mr. Walker was selling barrels of them to some stores, and he was preparing more to take to the Apple Festival down in Winston-Salem.

He told Mommy that if she wanted to cook up a bunch of jars of apple butter, he would take them up to the festival and sell them for her. That big unpainted house smelled like apples and cinnamon ever since he said that.

The apple orchard did seem like it would make a good secret garden, and it would surely hide us from being easily spotted by Mommy just in case she needed me. By the time we parted, Ruby and I had all sorts of plans for the afternoon.

When we got home, Mommy was on the porch peeling and cutting up apples. She was rocking and singing while she dropped the pieces into a big pot of water. She looked plenty busy, so I figured my plans would work out just fine.

I tried to slip around the side of the house, but Mommy jumped up from her apples and scurried down off the porch. Wiping her hands on her apron, she hollered, "I just have a few hours of daylight left, and that wind smells like it's a-gonna bring in a storm."

I looked up at the clear sky, not a cloud in sight. Celia was doing the same. As if reading our minds, Mommy said, "I can feel it in my bones. You'll see."

Right away, she put Rae to work getting her pot of apples to start cooking in the kitchen. "I need somebody to go and feed the animals while I get Ol' Rosie milked," she said, "and somebody else to pull in all that laundry off the line."

The laundry could be done in a hurry, but feeding the animals would take a while, especially because Mommy would probably want somebody to stay with her until she finished milking Ol' Rosie.

"I'll get the laundry!" I shouted. The only problem was, Celia shouted it at the same time. Mommy stopped and looked at both of us.

"Dahlia's not very tall, Mommy. She'll have trouble keeping that laundry off the ground." Celia looked at me with evil satisfaction. "Besides, I have homework to do!"

"Child, you have the whole weekend--" Mommy began, but I didn't waste any time.

"Mommy, those chickens scare me when they're hungry," I mumbled. I squeezed my eyes hard, trying to rustle up something close to a teardrop. "And the slop bucket is heavy. It's hard for me not to spill it before I get to the hog pen." I tilted my head to the side and did my best to look forlorn. "Besides, Charlie put the step-stool out by the line. I can pull it along and let the clothes drop into the basket. I've got it all worked out."

My pity show worked! Mommy said, "Celia, put your things inside and come on out to the barn with me." Celia's face turned white.

I ran toward the house before Mommy could change her mind (and before Celia could catch me). I threw my books on the chair and grabbed Daisy Rae. Then I hopped back down the stairs, two steps at a time, and picked up the big laundry basket. It was woven out of poplar strips, so it was light as a feather.

I ran past Rae, stirring apples and humming a

tune, and let the screen door slam behind me as I jumped off the stoop. Then I froze. Long, solid walls of laundry stretched out before my eyes. Mommy must have been scrubbing on that washboard all morning long. There were bed sheets, some of Poppy's work shirts, dresses, pants, an apron, and a couple of Mommy's skirts.

I decided to start with the biggest pieces first. The warm sun and fall gusts had worked their magic. The sheets felt crisp to touch, and they floated on the wind like clouds come down to earth. I dragged the step-stool under the first sheet, then climbed and stretched to pull the clothespins loose, letting each drifting cloud drop softly into the basket below.

Ordinarily, I'd get Rae to help me with folding. In the interest of hurrying, though, I decided to fold each sheet myself. They weren't neat, and I let the ends drag the ground a couple of times, but they were stacking up nicely. After the sheets, I tackled the pants and work shirts. Finally, I let the dresses, skirts, and apron lay over the top of the heap and tucked Daisy Rae into one side.

"Boo!" Ruby had come sneaking up behind me and made me jump so that I nearly toppled the basket of laundry.

"Hey, Ruby," I said, out of breath. "All I need to do is get this inside and we can go play. Help me lift it, okay?"

Ruby grabbed one side and I held the other. "Oh, it's so heavy," she grunted. We hurried toward the house with quick, small steps. My memory flashed back to carrying that five-gallon keg up from the spring. I wondered if Ruby knew how heavy water could be. I'm sure she didn't.

We opened the back door and set the basket just inside the kitchen. "Do you need help folding the sheets, Dahlia?" Rae called over her shoulder without even turning from the bubbling, boiling pot of apples.

"No, it's all done!" I hollered. I grabbed Daisy Rae and scooted outside, letting the screen door slam behind me once again.

Ruby was already running toward the apple orchard, so I raced to catch up with her. She took me by surprise with a sharp turn toward the windbreak along the orchard's edge. She wove her way through the sturdy oaks until suddenly, without warning, Ruby stopped. She stared up into the canopy of colorful leaves and whispered, "This is where we unlock the gate to Misselthwaite Manor's secret garden."

Just above Ruby's head, a branch reached down low enough to touch. "It's begging us to climb aboard," she shouted. "Come on! We'll pretend we're sitting atop the garden wall!"

Ruby gripped Lucille between her teeth, brown curls and flapping eyelids dangling, and hoisted herself up onto the low-reaching limb. "There's a little knob you can hold to steady yourself while you climb!"

I tried to hold Daisy Rae's arm between my teeth, but right away I gagged. "Toss her up!" Ruby said. I flung Daisy Rae toward her. Ruby caught the doll with one hand. She wobbled a little but stayed on the branch. I grabbed the limb and swung myself up beside Ruby, holding tight and trembling just a little.

"Master Craven is away, and Mrs. Medlock will never find us here," Ruby said, continuing the game.

Our pretend world seemed locked away from me for the moment. I struggled to keep still while my insides turned and trembled. Not Ruby. She balanced without even using her hands and swung her feet back and forth like leaves in the afternoon breeze.

"Dickon will be bringing seeds and garden tools

soon," Ruby said. "Perhaps we should start pulling weeds over there to prepare for planting flowers." She gestured toward a patch of earth shadowed by apple trees. I turned to look but kept both hands glued to the limb.

"Who do you want me to be?" I asked. We hadn't really discussed our parts.

"Oh, I guess that was rude of me to just plan on being Mary. Do you mind being Martha? We can pretend they found the garden together. It doesn't have to be just like the book."

"Okay, Mary." I leaned back into the crook of the tree and steadied myself against its jagged trunk. I stretched one leg out toward Ruby and locked the other around the limb.

"Oh, Martha," Ruby said, "you have the slightest hole forming on the bottom of your right shoe."

I tilted my foot and strained to see. There *was* a hole starting to form. I didn't know how I was going to hide that from Mommy. She'd worry right off that my feet wouldn't stay warm and dry. *If you let your feet get cold, you're sure to get sick.* That's what Mommy always said. On cold nights, she'd heat an iron, wrap it in thick cloth, and tuck it under the covers by our feet. That's how worried she got about our feet.

"Well, Mary," I said, trying to act like it was nothing, "these are my gardening shoes, of course."

Ruby giggled and so did I, but my mind started thinking about the book. Mary and Martha acted friendly enough, but Mary's uncle was the one who owned everything, and Martha was just there because she *worked* for him.

"I think Lucille is ready for a nap," Ruby said. "And we have work to do in the garden." She stretched up to the branch above us and found a safe spot for Lucille. "These tangled leaves and twigs can be a hammock, like in *Robinson Crusoe*!" Ruby announced with delight. "My Papa read that book to me! Do you know it?"

I'd never admit to Ruby that my Poppy didn't even know how to read. "I think Daisy Rae is sleepy too," I said, ignoring her question. I stretched as best I could with one hand still clinging to the tree. My legs shivered as I pushed Daisy Rae into the mess of twigs and leaves above my head. Then I clung to the trunk as I worked my way down behind Ruby.

Once my feet reached solid ground, the shivers eased away. We scooted leaves around and pulled up any little sprouts that looked like they were weeds. Then Ruby said, "Oh, let's take some sticks and form a big square fence! It can be our rose bed!" So that's what we did. Then she said, "Let's stick some leaves in the ground so they'll stand up. They can be young seedlings just beginning to grow." So we did that, too.

It was tiring work, actually. So I was not disappointed when we heard Ruby's momma clanging the iron dinner bell to call her home.

"I have to go," Ruby said. She swung herself back up on the branch and pulled Lucille into the crook of her arm. Ruby's hands were covered with dirt, which was an unusual sight.

"Maybe we can finish the game tomorrow," I offered.

"Oh, I'm busy tomorrow," Ruby answered. "Momma said we're going into town to shop for a new winter coat before the weather gets cold. Rosie just got a new brown coat. I hope I can find one just like it!" She turned to go, smiling from ear to ear.

That old knot twisted itself up in my stomach as Ruby skipped away. I knew I should get home. But I just stood there, staring at our pretend rose garden. It was nothing but an ugly mess of sticks and leaves, really. The cool wind blew a chill across my back and I longed for a new brown coat to keep me warm.

That's when the knot dropped into my feet and forced them to move. I kicked our sorry rose garden. I kicked and stomped and jumped up and down. I grunted and yelled and tried to send that knot bursting through the trees and into the sky.

And then I stopped. Everything was quiet. I stood frozen in the pretend rose bed I'd destroyed, counting my pounding heartbeats until they were carried away by the fast-moving wind. Suddenly, I wanted to make it right. My hands smoothed the dirt, and I tried to push the leaves back into their tidy rows. But the wind worked against me. It lifted and pushed and swirled my leaves into a sorry mess.

Soon I heard my name in that wind. It was Mommy's voice. I jumped up and ran for the house. Strong gusts of wind whipped at me the whole way and soft drizzles of rain stuck to my face.

"Dahlia, child, why'd you go wandering off? Didn't I tell you a storm was a-coming? Where were you?" I had barely stepped inside the house and Mommy was sending a flurry of questions my way. I couldn't think up any good answers and tried to hurry through the kitchen. But then I stopped. Celia and Rae were standing in the parlor, refolding all the sheets.

"I guess I didn't get those sheets folded good enough?" I mumbled.

"Wash those hands and help your sisters get those sheets folded proper."

I sunk my hands into the wash bucket and watched dirt lift itself into swirls of brown in the clear water. Mommy held her apron out for me to dry my hands, and then firmly turned my shoulders and gave me a little shove toward the parlor.

Celia reached toward me with one end of a sheet, and my breath caught in my throat. The lower part of her arm and back of her hand were lined with deep cuts that looked like they'd just stopped bleeding.

I took the sheet and caught her eyes for just a second. They were puffy and red, and her cheeks were stained with dried-up tears. She turned away, grabbed her book, and hurried up the stairs.

"What happened to her hand?" I whispered.

"That old rooster attacked her," Rae said. "I reckon she was trying to rush, and she went and made him mad. She's real worried about that book report. Teacher says she'll end up moving back a grade if she can't do a better job of gettin' her work done. Turns out this book report is something extra she can do so she won't get a failing grade."

Rae could've been a detective. She had such a way of finding out the story behind everything going on. We continued to fold in silence. I couldn't stop the picture in my head. Over and over, I saw that big rooster with his dark feathers and sharp claws.

"Children, make sure you're a-washed up and ready to eat!" Mommy called from the kitchen.

"But Mommy–," Celia's pitiful sob came from above. It was a sound I'd never heard her make.

"Not you, Celia, honey. You don't need any more water on that hand. Come on and eat a bite of supper," Mommy said softly. Poppy and Charlie shuffled in through the back door and I heard Mommy quietly explaining what had happened.

They kept their voices low, but I caught enough to know what they were talking about. I heard Poppy mention words like *Doc Blanchard* and *money,* and Mommy say things like *cleaning, infection,* and *wait and see.*

All through supper, Mommy kept Celia next to her, rubbing her back and pulling her close. Poppy lit the kerosene lamp, and the glow from its flame flickered and reflected off Celia's right arm. I tried not to look at it, but the harder I tried, the more I felt tempted to stare. Her right arm. The one she used for writing. How would she ever get that book report done now?

When supper was finished, Rae said she'd like to help Celia with her homework. Right away, I offered to clean up the kitchen. Mommy told Charlie to give me a hand, but I told him I didn't need help.

I wanted to be alone. And finally, I was. Shadows swayed in the flickering light and raindrops tapped on the tin roof. I tried to follow their rhythm as I washed, dried, and put away every dish – even the heavy iron skillet. Then I stood at the screen door and watched the misty rain fall through the twilight.

Every once in a while, a gust of wind would blow cool raindrops through the screen. The hair around my face had beads of water clinging to it. Even though I looked straight forward, I could see them dangling off to each side, holding on, not falling.

Suddenly, I didn't want to be alone anymore. I wanted someone to pull *me* close and rub *my* back. That's when I thought about Daisy Rae. I turned, trying to remember where I'd left her. And then the horrible thought struck me like a bolt of lightning. Daisy Rae was still in that oak tree, cradled in the crook of a high limb. I wanted to cry, but that wouldn't bring her back.

I was still alone. No one would know if I just ran out the back door and went to find her. I could be back before they even knew I was gone.

X

The gusts of wind were stronger than before, and the raindrops seemed large and almost angry. As I sloshed through mud, big drops fell through the trees and plopped down on my head, in my eyes, across my back. My feet struggled to grip the slick ground, and mud oozed through the little hole in my right shoe.

"Daisy Rae!" I sobbed. "I'm so sorry, Daisy Rae!" My tears mixed with rain. The sky grew darker as a gray blanket of clouds blotted out the setting sun.

I stopped along the windbreak, searching for that particular oak tree with the long, low limb spread out to one side. The shadow of darkness and gray blur of rain wrapped around me like walls closing in. Walls that separated me from poor Daisy Rae.

Why didn't I bring the lantern? Why did it have to rain? Why did I have to be so forgetful? Why couldn't this be a dream? My thoughts were doing nothing to help, but they echoed over and over in my mind.

I wished I could move time backward. I'd start over right at the point where Celia wanted to get the laundry. I'd let her do it. Or maybe I could go back to when Ruby's dinner bell rang. If only I had gotten Daisy Rae then and headed home. It was my fault. It was all my fault.

My thoughts swirled around like a whirlpool. I heard my own sobs over the drumming rain and howling wind. If I ever planned to find that tree with the low branch, I had to calm down.

I forced my eyes to stop crying and marched forward under the swaying oak limbs. They looked so different weighed down by the rain and covered in shadows.

Suddenly, wet leaves dropped from a limb sweeping low above my head. I stopped and looked up. The limb was close enough to touch. It was the tree that held Daisy Rae. It had to be.

I jumped, grabbed the limb, and swung my left foot up. I felt for the stepping knob and growled at the fear that tried to hold me back. My foot slid three times along the slick bark until it finally caught on the knob. I stretched tall and reached for the higher limb while my sloshy right foot braced itself against the trunk. Finally, I was getting somewhere.

I reached blindly into the crook of that limb. It was empty. My eyes crawled along the limb, blinking away tears and raindrops. And then my heart leapt. I saw a yellow glow dangling way down at the end. It was Daisy Rae. She was held in a thick tangle of twigs and leaves, pushed there by the slanted, angry rain.

I pulled myself up into the empty crook of that high limb and held on tight. I was able to see her dress now. Shredded fabric was woven into the mess of leaves and twigs. Wet cotton stuffing was seeping through her seams, and her limp arms and legs seemed to be pulling away from her body. I had to save her.

Inch by inch, I scooted along the thinning limb. At about the halfway point, I stretched my arm as long as it would go. "Daisy Rae," I whispered, "I'm so sorry, Daisy Rae." She was so close to my fingertips. I stretched a little more. A little more.

Suddenly, two sounds happened, and I'm not sure which came first. I thought I heard my name somehow, traveling across the wind. I looked toward the pasture and saw a small light bobbing up and down, up and down, like an oversized firefly.

The other sound was a loud clap of thunder that

shook a terrible tremor straight down into my heart. And just like that, the limb broke loose from the tree. That limb, Daisy Rae, and me – we all plunged through the darkness.

And that's the last thing I remember from that terrible day.

XI

My eyes ached and wanted to stay closed, but something in me felt determined to open them. Maybe I was curious. Maybe I was scared. But whatever it was, I'm glad I forced them open.

The room was thick with a fuzzy haze. In the corner, a rocking chair swayed back and forth, back and forth. It was Mommy. I locked my eyes on her and tried to focus. She wore her white dress with the faded pink flowers. I knew that dress well. And it made me feel safe.

I wanted to say something, but I couldn't remember how to make the words come out. Mommy had a crochet hook in her hands. A basket at her side. A ball of blue yarn.

Suddenly, she lifted her face. Her eyes found mine. She tossed the needlework aside and leapt out of the chair. It rocked wildly behind her.

"Rae, get your Poppy!" she hollered. "Dahlia's awake!"

Mommy's eyes filled with tears. She put a hand

on either side of my face. She smiled. And my heart ached.

Soon, Poppy was at the door. He wore a thick brown overcoat and carried his hat in his hands. "You're a sight for sore eyes," he told me. "I was beginning to think... well, I don't know what I was beginning to think...." His voice trailed off.

Mommy lifted a water glass to my lips, and the empty space in the room began to fill. Rae sat at the foot of the bed, humming and grinning. Charlie stood by Poppy and half-smiled, all pale and misty-eyed.

My arms felt empty. I reached for Daisy Rae but couldn't find her. "Daisy Rae?" I mumbled, mostly to myself. Everyone looked down at the floor. Except for Rae.

Rae's face got extra soft. "By the time Charlie found you, there was nothing left of Daisy Rae. Just some shredded fabric and soggy stuffing," she said quietly. "I'm sorry, Dahlia."

The rain. The limb. Daisy Rae. All at once, the memory played like a nightmare. *The light bobbing up and down. My name being carried on the wind.* It was Charlie. He was searching for me. And he found me.

I wanted to scream, but no sound came. Instead,

there was just pain. It started in my chest and traveled through me like muddy water. I wanted to run, but my body wouldn't move.

Then I looked toward the bedroom door, and there was Celia. She leaned against the doorjamb, half inside and halfway out. Her face held no meanness. Only worry and regret. I knew that feeling because worry and regret filled me up inside.

I wanted so badly to tell her I was sorry. I wanted to tell her that I'd been wrong. I wanted to tell her that if I could go back and make things different, I would. I tried to speak. The only word that came out was "Celia."

As soon as her name left my lips, Celia pulled herself away from the doorjamb and walked toward me. Her brown eyes were misty with tears. Poppy and Charlie parted like the Red Sea as she pulled herself to my side. I reached my hand up and she took it. Her scratches were still there, but they were beginning to heal. We just held onto each other's hands like that, and again, no words were necessary. She knew everything I wanted to say. And she was saying the same thing right back to me.

❋ ❋ ❋

Doc Blanchard said it'd be several weeks before I was ready to get out and about. But it was clear I wouldn't be lonely. Within just a day or two of me waking up, Miss Bessie and Ruby came to see me.

"Oh, you precious girl! Dahlia, it is so good to see those pretty blue eyes of yours!" Miss Bessie filled the doorway with her little round body and great big smile. In her hands, she held something that looked delicious.

"This is a seven-layer cake I made for you. I know it's your favorite, and I asked your Momma just how she makes it. Now, it might not be as good as hers, but it's made with lots of butter, lots of sugar, and lots of love." Her eyes glimmered with sweet tears, and the cake she held was beautiful. But what excited me most was seeing Ruby peeking out from behind her.

"All right now, sweet girl, I'm gonna go put this in the kitchen. I also brought over a mess of fried chicken, some good, warm beans, and a cake of cornbread. I just wanted you to see the special treat that's waiting for you once you eat up some of that food that's meant to make you strong!" She walked over to the bed and held the cake aside while she leaned down to kiss my forehead.

"Now Ruby has some things for you." She turned, still holding the cake out to the side by her left shoulder. "Not too much today, Ruby." Then she bustled off with the seven-layer cake.

Ruby's face looked like a mix of happy and scared. A cloth bag hung from her arm. She swallowed hard before coming out with some words. "Dahlia, are you okay? Doc Blanchard said you hit your head real hard on the ground. He wasn't sure if you'd wake up, or if you'd even be the same if you did."

That was the first anyone had told me of what the doctor said. Ruby grinned. "Doc Blanchard also said you must have the strongest bones in all of Forsythe County, because you didn't break a single one even though you hit the ground hard fallin' out of that tree."

A deep, muffled voice came from the doorway behind Ruby. "She's just got hard bones to go with that hard head." Charlie stood there holding a plate of food. "Mommy said you can eat in here 'cause you're not supposed to get out of the bed and walk around yet."

I hadn't realized I was hungry, but when I smelled cornbread and saw a pat of butter melting on top of it, my stomach started to rumble. A chicken leg sat next to it because Mommy knew that was my favorite.

While I sat there and ate, Ruby started unloading her cloth bag and telling me all about it. There was a slate and some chalk for me to continue practicing my writing and arithmetic. And of course, there was that reading primer book with all the word lists, sentences, and little stories.

"We will just do some review in that book," Ruby said. "Miss Coombs put the McGuffey First Reader in the bag. She expects you'll be ready to do some *real* reading soon, and I agree!"

The last and best thing Ruby pulled out of that bag was *The Secret Garden.* She said Miss Coombs had finished reading it to the class, but she marked the spot where I had left off listening.

Ruby said, "Miss Coombs told me she knows you will catch up on all your learning once I get to working with you every day."

"Every day?" I asked.

"Yes, Dahlia!" Ruby answered with a little pride in her voice. "Miss Coombs is not about to let you go all these weeks without any schoolwork. And neither am I!"

"Yes, ma'am," I replied. In the quiet of my heart,

I felt more than a little bit of satisfaction knowing that Ruby and I would be spending so much time together.

And so it began that Miss Ruby Walker became the best teacher and most loyal friend a girl could have. After school each day, she hurried to eat her snack and finish up her homework lessons. Then, Miss Bessie would pack up a snack for me, and Ruby would head on over with that little cloth bag.

To begin with, she sat in a straight back chair next to the bed. After a week or so, I was allowed to come downstairs and we worked in the parlor. Some afternoons, when it wasn't too cold, Mommy would even let us sit out on the front porch if we promised to stay bundled up and sit in the sunshine.

I think I learned more during those weeks than I'd ever learned in school. Ruby was serious about our lessons, but she had a way of making learning fun. She would imitate Miss Coombs and would sometimes even imitate Miss Eunice Dill. That probably wasn't nice, but even Charlie had to laugh when he saw how she did it.

Ruby pinched her nose up tight like she was trying to squeeze it between her squinted eyes. She drew up her lips and squeaked out in a high-pitched voice, "Pupils, you will open your McGuffey Primer to page forty. Practice reading each word and take care to articulate both consonant and vowel sounds exactly as we have reviewed. Please proceed."

It felt like we were playing, but pretty soon reading was coming naturally to me. All those words and sentences started dancing together into stories that came to life.

This house is on fire.
Look, the roof is in a blaze.
Run, boys, and ring the bell.

I pictured flames leaping off the rooftop and felt a shiver of fear. I had to remind myself it was only a story. I was amazed that reading could become so real. I was waking up again, but this time my mind was waking up in a whole new way.

Once we finished the reading primer, we started right in on the first reader. We came to a page that said:

The old cow is in the pond: see her drink!
Will she not come out to get some grass?
No, John, she likes to be in the pond.

As soon as I read that one, Ruby said, "Well,

John, it's gonna be quite a job to milk that cow!" And we giggled until our sides hurt.

In that moment, my world felt good and clean and right. For so many months, I had been a little bird tossed about in a strong wind. But in that moment, the wind was calm and my world was right.

Ruby wasn't my only teacher. Rae read to me every evening from *The Secret Garden* like Miss Coombs intended, but she was already so burdened. On top of Miss Dill's homework assignments, Mommy needed Rae's help with the ironing and the cooking and the cleaning.

One evening after supper, Celia climbed up in the bed beside me with *The Secret Garden* in her hands. She started talking without looking at me. "I already know what happens, so I'll try not to give away any secrets," she said. "It looks like Rae left off here at the part where the children want to take that little sick boy to the garden. So now the doctor is going to come to the house and visit, but don't trust him 'cause— Well, never mind. Just listen."

Celia began to read. Beautiful words flowed from her lips one after another like a song. Like she was back singing on the flat rock, not even having to think about the words. Just singing the story right out loud. And when Celia sang the words, the book came to life.

I could see Master Craven and Misselthwaite Manor and Mary and the garden all so clearly. People who lived like Mr. John D. Rockefeller. I could see their golden walls and trinkets and toys, their fine clothes, fancy rooms, and feasts. And I could also see their slumped shoulders, shadowy faces, and sad eyes.

"Celia," I interrupted. "Why do you think these people are so miserable? They've got everything a person could want."

"Well," Celia began. She closed the book and marked the page with a thin red ribbon. "I guess they're just so lonesome for Colin's momma. Losin' her just left a big hole in their hearts and they couldn't seem to get over it."

"How was it she died?" I just couldn't remember.

Celia's voice was quiet and careful. "She was in the garden. And she fell from a tree."

An awful chill went down my spine, and my fingers and toes turned to ice. I needed to say something, but my mind wasn't sure just what that something was.

I looked up at Celia, and she was smiling down

at me. The kind of smile that looked sad and happy at the same time. The kind of smile that softened her whole face and put a warm glow in the cold room.

"Celia, I'm so sorry," I told her. And I think she understood. She didn't make a face or roll her eyes or even say a word. She just put her arms around me, and her hug said all the words I ever needed to hear.

XII

November was almost over, and the ground was ankle-deep with crunchy leaves. The air was downright chilly – not just in the morning and evening, but all day long. And as the weather got colder, I got stronger. Doc Blanchard said I should be ready to go back to school after Christmas.

"In the meantime," he told me, "I want you to get up and walk – no running or jumping – walk around as much as you can." He could've stopped right there, but for some reason he looked at Mommy and added, "A few chores might be a good idea, Mrs. Harrell."

The very next day, Mommy handed me a basket and sent me out to collect the eggs. "The hens aren't a-laying like they used to," she said, "but make sure you check every nest. We don't want to let any eggs spoil." She bundled me up in Celia's old blue coat, wrapped a scarf around my head and neck, and pushed me out the door. I strolled out to the henhouse watching my breath make little clouds in the cold air.

When I unlatched the big wooden door, light flooded the coop. Right away, six chickens waddled up and cackled in circles all around my feet. And they left their eggs right out in the open. "Well, thanks for making it easy, girls." I figured talking kindly while I stole their eggs might make this whole ordeal seem a little friendlier.

The rest of the eggs were not so easy. Three hens stayed put on their nests. I started with the smaller two. I took a deep breath and half-sang in a high-pitched voice, "Hey, pretty little hen. I just need to reach down here and get these eggs." After just a little jostling, they scooted off their boxes.

The last one was a big black broody hen spread out flat on her box. I used the high-pitched, sing-songy voice, but I changed the words. "Hey, you ol' stubborn ugly sack of feathers." She turned her head sideways and one black eye stared at me. "That's right, scoot along now." She stayed put.

I set the pail down by my feet, stretched up tall, and put my hands on my hips. "Only one of us is a chicken," I told her, "and it's not me!" I picked that big broody hen up with my two hands and set her on ground. She flapped her wings and cackled, but that was it. One by one, I pulled five eggs from that nest. And then I thanked her kindly.

Just as I was about to march back to the house in triumph, that mean old rooster met me at the door to the chicken coop. He scratched the ground with his sharp claws and pranced back and forth with his chest puffed out and his head held high.

My heart pounded and my knees trembled, but I knew what I had to do. I stood tall and puffed my chest up just like that rooster. I waited until he pranced to the left, and then I marched boldly to the right, holding the pail between us like a shield.

He hollered out and jumped at me, but I pushed the pail toward him and yelled, "Get on out of here!" like I'd heard Mommy do. And it worked! That old rooster pranced his way into the coop and I kept on walking. But I felt like dancing.

Mommy and I did most of our work in the mornings. Then we bundled up and sat on the porch in the afternoons to watch for my brother and sisters coming home from school. Of course, Mommy always worked while she sat. She shelled beans, peeled potatoes, cracked walnuts...anything to keep busy. I rocked along beside her, and practiced with my slate and chalk.

One afternoon, Mommy brought a basket full of mending out on the porch. She worked her needle in and out, putting a new hem in the bottom of Charlie's trousers. She stopped for a minute and said, "Dahlia, your writin' is a-getting so neat. I bet you could handle a needle and thread."

Sewing was something Rae did a lot and Celia did sometimes, but no one had ever shown me how to work a needle and thread. She pulled out one of Poppy's shirts that had come apart along a seam and turned it inside out. "See how these two pieces of fabric line up together?"

I nodded.

She squinted her eyes and pushed white thread through the eye of the needle. Then she knotted the end by circling thread around her finger, rolling it off, and pulling it tight. I watched her hands guide the needle back and forth through the layers of fabric, making tight, straight stitches.

I'd never watched her hands so closely before. I'd never noticed the brown spots sprinkled across her skin or the way her knuckles bulged slightly and made her fingers look just a little crooked.

"You think you could handle that, Dahlia?" Her voice startled me.

"I guess so," I told her, "as long as you think I won't make a mess of Poppy's shirt."

"Oh child, I wouldn't give you a shirt just yet."

She laughed like I had said something funny. "You can have a couple of scraps to work with until you get to going real good."

She pulled out two strips of faded blue fabric. "Match up the right sides, and I'll thread the needle for you," she told me. "Let's see if you can stitch a straight line from one end to the other."

I worked the needle in and out, just like Mommy had done, but my stitches were crooked and all different sizes. Mommy said, "That's it. You just keep a-practicin'."

And so the chilly December days passed quietly, with me churning butter, collecting eggs, practicing my sewing, and learning just about everything else there was to know from Ruby in the afternoons.

The last day of school before the Christmas holiday, my sisters came home skipping and singing. Even Charlie had a little spring in his step.

As soon as Mommy heard us walk into the house, her voice trilled like birdsong. "Christmas is a-comin', and that means there's plenty of chores to go 'round." Only Mommy could make chores sound like something to be excited about.

The Walkers invited us to a big Christmas Eve dinner at their house. Miss Bessie said she'd cook the meat, cornbread, and some cinnamon apples.

Mommy planned to take a big pot of beans and a black walnut cake. She put Charlie to work out in the barn, cracking black walnuts with a hammer.

Rae was sewing a cushion for Mommy's porch rocker as a Christmas gift, and she worked on it every free minute she could find. Most of the time, it stayed hidden under her mattress. The top of it looked like a log cabin quilt square, with long colorful strips made from all different scraps. One night, while she was sitting on her bed sewing on her secret, I showed Rae some of the sewing I'd been practicing. My stitches were nowhere near as tight as hers, but they were improving.

When Rae saw my needlework, she raised her eyebrows and dropped her mouth open. "Dahlia," she said, "instead of all this practicing, do you wanna make something you can enjoy?"

"I don't want to make quilts, Rae." I said it as politely as I could.

"No," she laughed. Then she touched my arm gently and said, "Would you like to make a doll?"

Thoughts of Daisy Rae swarmed into my mind. Thoughts I had locked out of my memory. They stung my insides like angry bees and made my eyes burn with hot tears.

Rae put a hand on my shoulder. "Daisy Rae was

made from scraps, just like we have here. All the love that went into her is something *you* put there. And you still have that love, Dahlia. You still have love to give."

Tears rolled to my chin and hung there, hesitating. "Rae, I can still see her in my mind. And it hurts. It hurts so bad."

Rae put her cushion aside and wrapped her arms around me. I sunk into her shoulder and sobbed. It was the first time I had really cried over Daisy Rae.

"I wish I could go back," I told Rae. "I wish I could go back and do that day all over again. What happened to Daisy Rae, and to me, and what happened to Celia – it's all my fault!"

Once that door inside me opened, those thoughts just came charging out. I was the cause of the worry in our house. I was the reason Daisy Rae was gone forever. Every bit of grief was my doing.

Rae's voice was soft but firm. "This is a new day, Dahlia. You can never change a thing going backwards. But you can always move ahead and make something new." She lifted my head off her shoulder and picked up her sewing basket. "That's why *you* need to make a new doll."

I was still reeling from the words that had

tumbled out of me, but Rae seemed to be saying the crying time was over. She took out some scraps and showed me what to do. I sat on the bed and cut the scraps into two sides of a doll's body. Then I sewed the right sides together almost all the way around.

The following night, Rae showed me how to stuff cotton into the body and sew it up from the outside. For the rest of that week, we worked in secret on our projects. I don't know why I was keeping mine a secret. It just seemed more fun that way. Of course, Celia knew what we were doing, but she didn't pay us any mind. She'd just crawl up into her bed with a book. That girl was determined to read.

For the finishing touches, Rae showed me how to attach buttons and yarn to make the face and hair. She was smaller than Daisy Rae, and not near as pretty, but I made that doll myself. Something about her seemed to set things right.

And that's when it all went wrong again. I don't understand why peace can't seem to stay in your heart but a minute before something comes along to stir it all up into a frenzy. I was sitting on the bed trying to think up a name for my new doll when Charlie came running up the stairs all out of breath.

"Poppy just heard," he said between gasps, "Zeke's cabin burned to the ground."

XIII

Just two days before Christmas, a light snow filled the air and dusted the ground. We were bundled up and huddled together on the front porch, watching the huckster truck slowly ramble up Salem Road, leaving long dark tracks behind it on the powdery ground.

When the truck turned onto the Walkers' farm, my eyes latched onto the back seat. From where I stood, I could see what looked like a snowy white beard peeking through the windshield. My heart knew it had to be Grandpap, and my spirit lifted like a dove in flight.

Mr. Walker had driven Poppy back to the mountain, to the home that no longer existed. Charlie went along to help clean up all the burned mess. Poppy promised he'd make Grandpap come back with them for the holiday. And somehow, he was able to pull that off.

The truck rolled slowly to a stop and we all stood there, not sure if we should move. Finally the engine cut off and doors began to creak open. Four tired, sad bodies eased out onto the cold, gray ground of the Walkers' farm.

Poppy walked toward Mommy. Silent tears rolled from her eyes before he even spoke a word. In a low, muffled voice he finally said, "Somebody set the fire. One of those wild Spicer boys was probably a-drinkin'. We'll never know for sure." He looked at her shoulder as he spoke. Mommy didn't say a word. She buried her face in Poppy's chest and sobbed quietly.

A million questions raced through my mind... *Was there anything left of our beds or the old wood-burning stove? What about the five-gallon water keg? Would the dahlias still come up in the spring?*

But my questions melted away when Grandpap wrapped his arms around me. "Oh my little July flower, your Poppy told me..." His voice trailed off and he squeezed a little tighter.

Just when I thought I couldn't hold back tears any longer, he released me and patted each one of us on the head. "Now you children help carry my things into the house. Let Charlie get that box. It's heavy." He pointed to a crate in the back of the truck. "And no peeking at what's inside!"

Charlie carried the box, along with an unfamiliar satchel hanging off one shoulder. I tried to catch his eyes, but he never looked up from the ground. I watched him trudge slowly up the front steps, shoulders slumped and head bowed, until he disappeared into the unpainted house.

Mr. Walker shook Poppy's hand and climbed back into his truck. The rest of us followed Charlie into the house. Rae put the oven fire out while Celia and I ladled hot chicken and dumplings into each bowl. Mommy sat down at the table, steam rising like a cloud in front of her empty face.

Poppy bowed his head and we all did the same. We sat there for a long minute, and then Poppy finally prayed. "Thank you, Lord, for what we've still got." That's all he said.

We waited another long minute, and finally Grandpap said, "Amen."

We dug into our food, and the only sound was the clanging of spoons against bowls. There were no words until Rae finally said, "It's delicious, Mommy."

We all nodded, and that seemed to open the door. After that, we asked Grandpap about the mountain and he asked us about our schooling. "I'm just happy to get a break from school," Celia said. That tickled Grandpap, and once he started, we all busted out laughing. Well, everybody except for

Charlie.

"May I be excused?" Charlie asked. His eyes stared into his empty bowl.

"Go on, son," Poppy said. "You could use a rest."

We listened as Charlie's heavy footsteps got quieter until they stopped in the attic room.

"He's had a rough go of it," Poppy said. He was talking to Mommy, but we all tuned in to listen.

"Just the chimney's left a-standin'. We cleaned up the charred rubble and salvaged what little might still be useful. Once we got the ground cleared, that boy started in on a-diggin' up every inch of dirt."

Mommy shook her head. "Not that treasure again," she said.

I couldn't help but look up at that point. Grandpap clapped his hands and changed the subject. "Let's get this kitchen cleaned up, and you children can take me out to see what kind of stars they have here in Lothian Mill."

Working all together, we got the kitchen cleaned up fast, but I didn't follow the others outside. As quietly as I could, I slipped away and climbed the steep staircase up to the attic. I knocked three times on the door.

"Come on in," Charlie's voice mumbled.

He was lying on the bed with his hands folded behind his neck. His bony elbows stuck out like wings on either side of his head.

"So you didn't find anything?" I asked.

He sat up when he realized it was me. Tears welled up in his eyes, and his disappointment was so strong I could almost smell it. "We'll never amount to anything, Dahlia," he said. He got off the bed and walked to the corner. That satchel he'd been carrying earlier was propped against the wall.

"Oh, I found that treasure, I guess, but it ain't worth nothin'." He opened the satchel and pulled out an old tin box. It was the sealed-up-tight kind of box people used for storing their important papers.

"I took a shovel, Dahlia. I knew if Ol' Zeke buried his fortune under that cabin, this was gonna be my chance to find it."

"That was smart thinking," I told him.

"I started at one end and dug my way to the other," he continued. I wasn't gonna let myself give up until I'd turned over every bit of soil." A beam of moonlight was shining in through that little attic window. Charlie's face looked like it was glowing with its own soft light as he looked down at the old tin box.

"You should be proud of yourself for trying," I told him. "Nobody else was willing to work so hard on the chance that story could be true."

"No one else is so foolish," he said. "When I reached the north end of the plot, I hit on metal, and I actually got excited." He stopped for a minute and swallowed hard. "I was already picturing that mansion. I figured we'd get an icebox. And store-bought clothes, of course. We could give all our clothes to poor children –" His voice trailed off.

"What's in the box?" I asked him.

Charlie opened up the lid and looked away. Inside, there was a quilt. It was yellowed and tattered, and starting to go to pieces, but there it was. A little pink and white quilt with a shoo-fly pattern. The quilt Juliette had made for baby Polly. That was Zeke's treasure. It was his heart, all folded up and stored in an old tin box.

XIV

Soft, silent snow kept coming down all through Christmas Eve morning. The others gathered in the kitchen, buzzing around and chattering like chickens. The beans were already cooking and Mommy was working on the cornbread. The sounds and the smells were more than I could handle. I eased out onto the porch, wrapped in a quilt, and watched whiteness slowly cover the gray winter earth. I held my new, nameless doll in my cold hands, trying to feed love into her.

After a while, Charlie came out and joined me. He brushed some snow off the top step and sat down, arms crossed and elbows leaning on his knees. He was perfectly still for a long time and just as silent as the snow.

I didn't mind the silence, but I felt like I should say something. I just didn't know what to say. I eased out of my chair and slid in next to him on the top step. Then I pulled my quilt around his shoulder until we were both wrapped up in it.

I don't know why, but I started to hum, and then

the words came.

> *"No home, no home, cried a little girl*
> *At the door of a rich man's home*
> *As she feebly leaned on a marble wall*
> *And stood on a polished stone."*

"Why do you think all those old songs are so sad and lonesome?" Charlie asked without looking up.

"I don't know," I said. "I reckon people don't have time to write songs when they're happy. Maybe they only sit still when they're sad and lonesome."

Charlie shrugged. "Makes sense, I guess."

Snow was sticking to the ground and the bushes and the trees. Little by little, it was making the world white. Wooden fence rails had little piles of snow lining along them like thin strips of icing in a seven-layer cake. The pole barn cast its shadow on the whiteness, and that green water pump looked like a soldier standing guard and keeping the peace.

Peace is what I felt. "Charlie..." I spoke gently. "What did you do with it?"

"For now, it's in the satchel Mr. Walker let me borrow."

"Are you going to keep it?"

Charlie stared off down the road. "I've been thinking about it. And I think the best thing to do is to take it back and bury it at the north end of the plot, just where Zeke had it. Put it back to rest. Mr. Walker said he'd take Grandpap back to the mountain when he's ready to go. I'll ride along and do it then."

"I think that's a good idea," I told him. "And Charlie?"

"Yeah?"

"Do you think you could dig up some dahlia bulbs and bring 'em back?"

He lifted his head and his eyes gazed upward like he was picturing those dahlias spread out and bursting with color in front of the unpainted house. "Hmm," he said, "maybe I should."

In the early afternoon, we gathered at the Walkers' house for our Christmas Eve dinner. I looked at the faces around me, all weary but smiling in spite of it. Everything we'd known was just a memory. But here we stood, old family and new friends, gathered together and sharing a meal. Talking and laughing and looking forward to Christmas Day.

After dinner, we cleaned up the dishes and played in the settling snow, tossing snowballs and making snow angels until Mommy and Miss Bessie made us stop and go put on warm, dry clothes. Even Grandpap put on his woolen Sunday coat and hat along with a scarf that had been made by the grandma I never knew.

Mommy let me carry my little nameless doll with me as we all walked together up to the church with two red doors. Dwight, Jr. sat with Charlie, but Ruby, Wayne, and Hoyt couldn't sit in the pews with us because they had parts in the pageant. Several children had been practicing so they could put on a silent show about the night Jesus was born. Ruby was playing an angel, and she had to cover her new Christmas dress with a long white robe.

The preacher told the story of Mary and Joseph being poor and traveling to Bethlehem. Two children walked up the aisle, covered in tattered cloth and trudging like they were tired. They met another child, playing the innkeeper, who shook his head as the preacher told us about there being no room.

"And then they went out to where the animals were kept," he said. I wondered if there were chickens, and I wondered if it snowed in Bethlehem.

The children pretending to be Mary and Joseph sat down next to the preacher. Then his voice got very excited and he said, "That night there were shepherds in the field!" Wayne and Hoyt shuffled down the aisle holding walking sticks. "And an angel of the Lord appeared to them!"

I had to raise up out of my seat to see Ruby, but there she was in her white robe, holding her arms out at her sides.

"Fear not!" the preacher said. And then he repeated, "Fear not. I bring you good news of great joy!" After that, he got real quiet and said, "That good news, my friends, is love. Love came down that night as a gift to you and me and all humankind. If we let love fill our hearts, there is no room for fear. Hear the good news," he said, "and fear not."

Then we all got to hold up candles and sing "Silent Night" together. Darkness crept up on the gray twilight outside, but in the church, there was plenty of light.

After the service, all the children lined up because the Ladies' Relief Society was handing out little brown bags. As we took our places in line, I looked around for Ruby. Suddenly I felt someone tapping me softly on the shoulder. I turned toward the tap, thinking it was Ruby, but instead I saw Ida. Her hair was still matted and her fingernails were still black, but she wore a pretty green dress, white stockings, and shiny black shoes. She smiled and said, "Merry Christmas, Dahlia. I missed you."

"Oh, Ida, I missed you too!" I said, suddenly realizing that Ida must've worked alone while I'd been gone. "I'm coming back to school as soon as it starts again," I told her.

Ida didn't seem excited. She just nodded quietly and said, "That's a pretty little dolly, Dahlia." We held hands all the way through the line. When we got to the front and the ladies handed our little brown bags to us, we both peeked inside right away. There was an apple, an orange, and a big peppermint candy stick.

"Oh, my!" Ida said, a delighted smile spreading across her face. "I don't believe I've ever had an orange before." I hadn't even thought about the orange, because I was concentrating on that peppermint candy stick. Those ladies sure knew how to make people happy.

As soon as we had cleared the line of children, Ida stopped. "Dahlia," she said, "I don't reckon I'll be seeing you once school starts back up. My daddy says we'll be moving up to Bluefield, West Virginia.

He's sure he can find some work there in the coal mines."

My eyes fought to hold back tears. Those prickling tears that remind you that you should have done something differently, but you'll never get the chance to go back and make it right.

Clear as day, I pictured Ida sitting alone at recess time. I could see her dry biscuit and sad eyes. I could hear her struggling to sound out words while I stewed over having to work with her.

But here was sweet Ida, probably wearing a dress from the Ladies' Relief Society, just like me. Here was sweet Ida, head bowed down low, hollow cheeks, and dark circles under her big brown eyes.

"Ida, I'm gonna miss you," I told her. And I meant it. "Here, take this." I pushed the little nameless doll into her hand. She tried to make me take it back, but I needed her to take it.

A low voice mumbled her name, and just before she turned to leave, Ida wrapped her arms around me in a big bear hug. "Thank you, Dahlia! That's just the nicest thing!"

And I couldn't say a word. All I could do was cry.

That night, when we got back to the house, we piled up together in the parlor and listened to

Grandpap tell stories about his peach trees and the cold spring water and Hugh Spicer. Poppy pulled out his banjo and we sang together – some Christmas songs and some old sad mountain songs – whatever Poppy knew how to play. We sang and we talked and we laughed until we could barely stay awake.

"You children best be a-gettin' on to bed now," Poppy said. Then he winked and added, "Ol' Santy Claus can't visit if you're awake." Celia, Rae, and Charlie shuffled up the stairs while Mommy and Poppy put out the lamps.

I watched Grandpap ease out the front door into the dark night. I wrapped a quilt around me like a tight cocoon and tiptoed out to stand beside him. A million stars twinkled above us, and the white blanket of snow on the ground shined with their reflection.

"I just need a little more time outside before I stay in for the night," he said without even looking to see who was standing beside him.

"Remember when I slept out with you, Grandpap?" I asked him.

"Well, of course I do, little Dahlia," he answered, his eyes still cast upward. "Too bad it's so cold. We can't sleep out tonight, for sure."

I thought back to the stars we saw sleepin' out on the mountain. It was amazing to think that the very same stars could be seen from both places at the same time. Zeke's chimney – the only thing left from his cabin – seemed so far away from the porch of this unpainted two-story house. But to the stars, it probably looked real close.

"I do believe my peaches turned out mighty fine this year," Grandpap said. "Don't go a-spoilin' my surprise, but I brought a whole crateful of candied peaches for a Christmas gift." I noticed the curl of a smile sneaking through his fuzzy white beard.

Grandpap and his peaches here on the Walkers' farm. My two worlds were coming together. And I smiled too.

"Grandpap," I said, "I don't think we're so very poor."

He put an arm around me and closed his eyes. I looked up at the snowflakes dancing silently in the moonlight. Grandpap whispered, "He's a-watchin' over us for sure." He squeezed my shoulder and I looked up to see a single tear on his wrinkled cheek.

Then I understood. It wasn't that old hoot owl watching over us that night. I had no reason to be afraid, then or now. I wrapped my arms around Grandpap's waist and closed my eyes. *If we let love fill our hearts, there is no room for fear.*

"Thank you," I whispered. It was the only thing I ever really needed to say.

Acknowledgements

This book has been a labor of love that has taken longer to write than I'd like to admit. However, it hasn't been a solitary venture. The seed of this story was planted long ago, and a community of loving supporters nurtured its growth and development along the way. I owe a great debt of gratitude to so many:

To my parents, for sharing the stories of their youth. They lived lives of struggle and conflict, grief and loss, love and joy – all the stuff of great stories. Although Dahlia and her story are completely fictional, the setting is built from my mother's childhood experience. Her family left their mountain cabin in the foothills of the Blue Ridge Mountains and moved to Rural Hall, North Carolina, where they lived and worked as tenant farmers for a few years. Before she passed away, my mother got to hear the very beginnings of Dahlia's story, and I will carry in my heart always the memory of her glistening eyes and satisfied smile as she listened.

To my sisters, for being lifelong supporters and encouragers of my creative endeavors. They never fail to show up and bring the joy. From school plays to county fair poetry readings to lengthy awards ceremonies, they cheered me on, lifted me up, and reminded me just how fortunate I was. And they still show up. For this book, I'm especially indebted to my sister Judy, who willingly and joyfully volunteered to be my beta reader. She has a keen eye for typos, and she knows more about Dahlia than anyone outside my own mind.

To my great big extended family. They know how to love, laugh, share, and stay connected. Their presence is constant in my heart, whether we are miles apart or all together in one place.

To my students at Holy Comforter Episcopal School in Tallahassee, Florida, for their enthusiastic willingness to listen and provide constructive feedback. Their unwavering faith sustained me in times of doubt. Every writer needs a critique group, and I cannot imagine a more honest and authentic band of writers and readers.

To my gracious friends and fellow writers who provided feedback. As I struggled for the right beginning, retired publisher Julia Graddy offered thoughtful guidance and sage advice. When my plot was stuck in the mud and I couldn't find a way out, author and mentor Jan Godown Annino helped me find my way forward. When the manuscript needed to be reworked and refined, M.R. Street asked all the right questions and provided the perspective I needed to make it right. When I wanted to know how readers would receive the story, my dear literature-loving friends, Rosanne Reanier and Sandra Wylie, dove into Dahlia's story and emerged with valuable observations and passionate assurance.

To my children, who fill my heart. When they were young, we shared books, songs, and laughter. Now they are adults, and we still share books, songs, and laughter. They impress me every day with their brilliance and inspire me with their creativity. They walk beside me and light the path to the future. Most importantly, they are good people who spread positive energy in this world.

To my grandchildren, who fill my spirit with joy. They are rainbows, painting gray days with colorful beauty and reminding me of the future's promise.

To my husband, John. He is my rock. He patiently endures my need for writing space, the reading lamp that stays on way too late at night, and the waves of emotion that accompany the process of writing, revising, querying, and waiting.

And finally, to young readers everywhere. Because of them, hope exists.

About the Author

Susan Koehler has been an educator for more than three decades and a writer for as long as she can remember. She has taught students from kindergarten to college, working to instill a love of reading and writing. Her earlier publications

include five non-fiction books for children and four professional development books on the teaching of writing. *Dahlia in Bloom* is her first work of fiction. Susan and her husband live in Tallahassee, Florida, where they enjoy outdoor activities, cooking, and spending as much time as possible with their five very busy children and two adorable grandchildren.

Contact Susan at www.susankoehlerwrites.com or www.turtlecovepress.com.

Additional Titles from Turtle Cove Press

Snowden's Story: One Marine's Indebtedness to the Corps
by Lt. Gen. Lawrence F. Snowden, USMC, Ret.

Blue Rock Rescue
by M.R. Street

The Werewolf's Daughter
by M.R. Street

The Hunter's Moon
by M.R. Street

LCRC Young Authors' Writing Contest 2016
Anthology

LCRC Young Authors' Writing Contest 2017
Anthology

Leon County Reading Council Young Authors' Writing Contest 2018
Anthology

Leon County Reading Council Young Authors' Writing Contest 2019
Anthology (coming Fall 2019)

Queen of the Clouds: Jerrie Mock and Joan Merriam Smith's Epic Quest to Become the First Woman to Fly Solo Around the World
by Taylor Phillips (coming soon)

Made in the USA
Columbia, SC
28 August 2019